GRAPHIC SCIENCE

THE *POWERFUL* WORLD OF
ENERGY

WITH

SUPER SCIENTIST

4D An Augmented Reading Science Experience

by Agnieszka Biskup | illustrated by Cynthia Martin and Anne Timmons

Consultant:
Christopher J. Conklin
Chemist, Aldrich Chemical
Member, American Chemical Society
Washington, D.C.

CAPSTONE PRESS
a capstone imprint

Graphic Library is published by Capstone Press,
1710 Roe Crest Drive, North Mankato, Minnesota 56003.
www.mycapstone.com

Library of Congress Cataloging-in-Publication Data is available on the Library of Congress website.

ISBN: 978-1-5435-5873-9 (library binding)
ISBN: 978-1-5435-6006-0 (paperback)
ISBN: 978-1-5435-5883-8 (eBook PDF)

Summary: In graphic novel format, follows the adventures of Max Axiom
as he explains the science behind energy.

Set Designer
Bob Lentz

Cover Artists
Tod G. Smith

Editor
Christopher Harbo

Book Designer
Alison Thiele

Colorist
Krista Ward

Photo Credits
Capstone Studio: Karon Dubke, 29, back cover; Shutterstock, 23

1. Ask an adult to download the app.

Capstone 4D
Education

2. Scan any page with the star.

3. Enjoy your cool stuff!

OR

Use this password at capstone4D.com

energy.58739

Printed in the United States of America.
PA48

TABLE OF CONTENTS

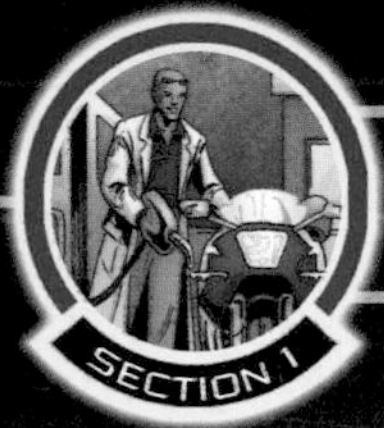
SECTION 1

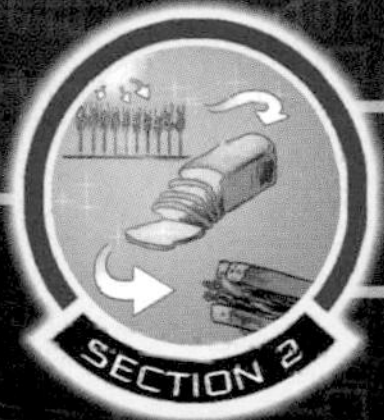
SECTION 2

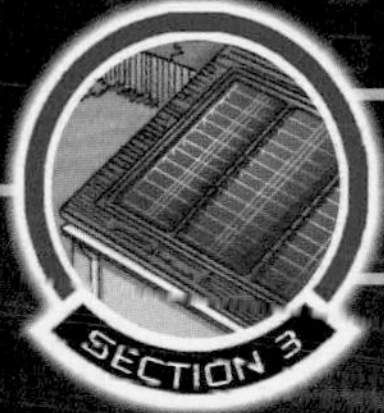
SECTION 3

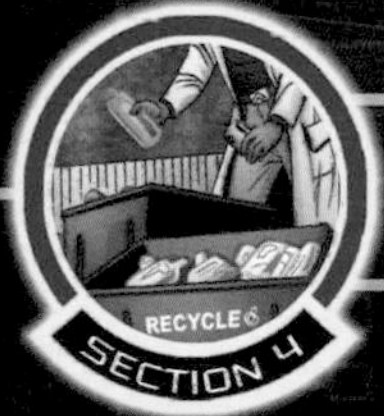
RECYCLE
SECTION 4

SECTION 1 WHAT IS ENERGY?

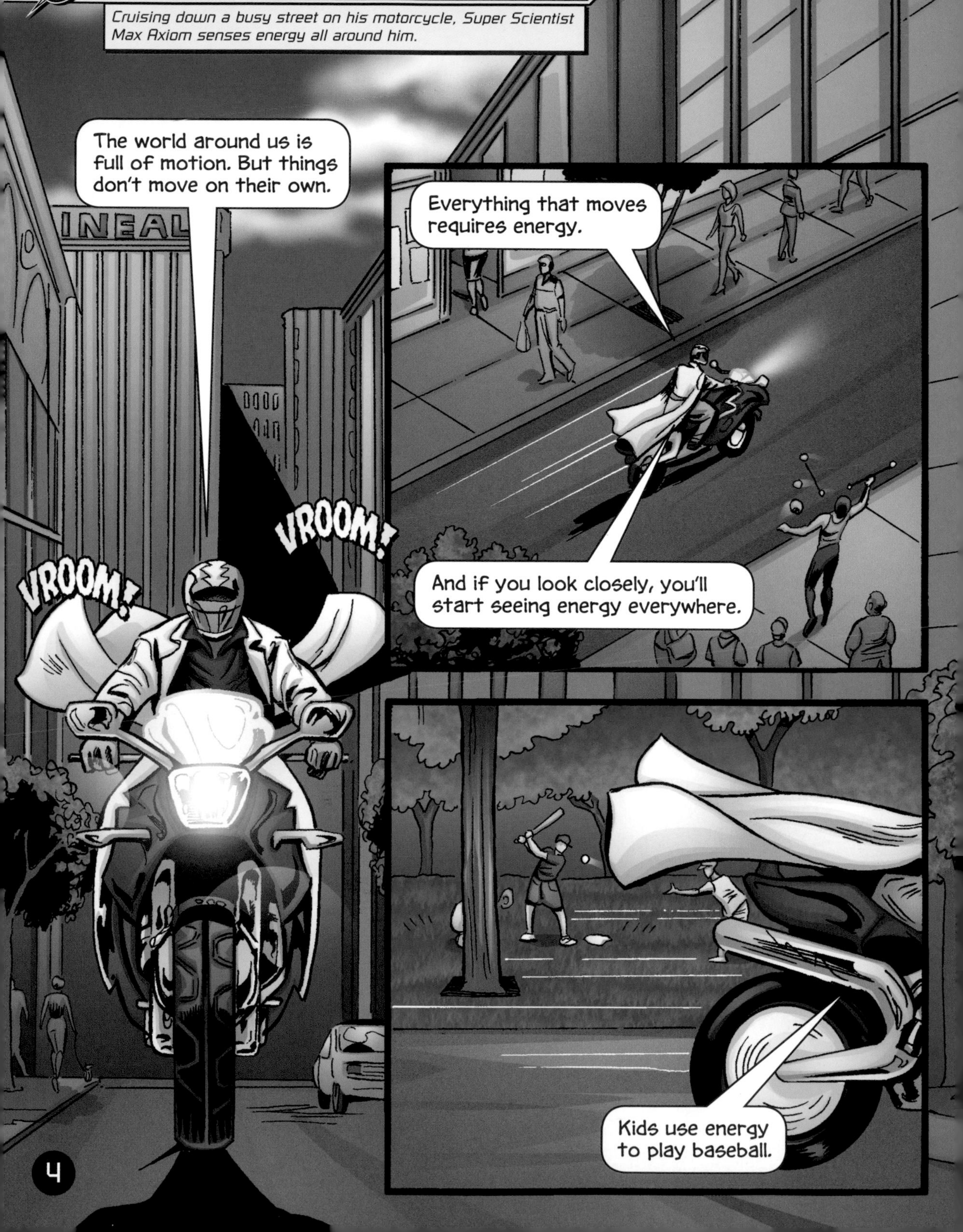
Cruising down a busy street on his motorcycle, Super Scientist Max Axiom senses energy all around him.
The world around us is full of motion. But things don't move on their own.
INEAL
VROOM!
VROOM!
Everything that moves requires energy.
And if you look closely, you'll start seeing energy everywhere.
Kids use energy to play baseball.

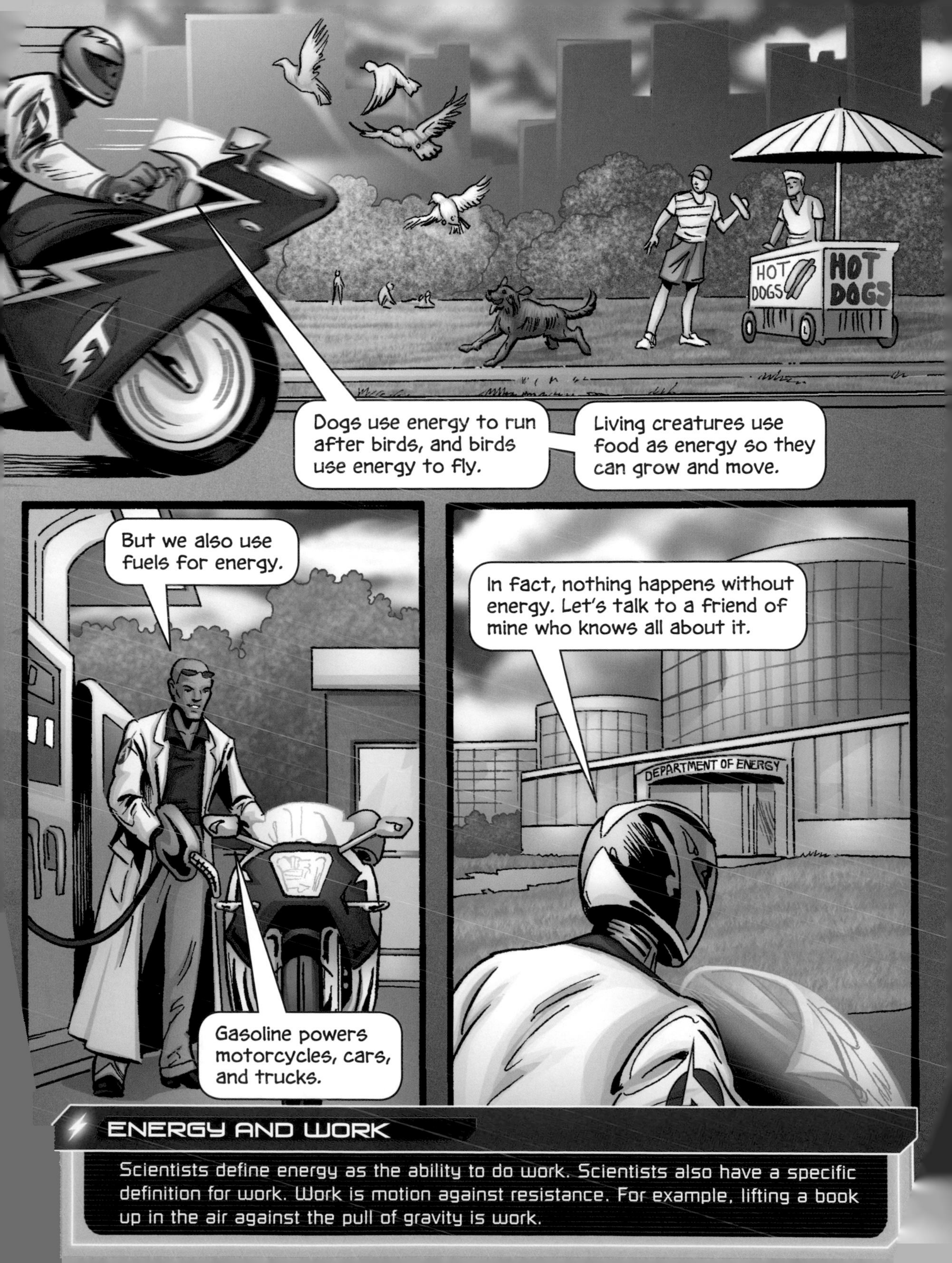
Dogs use energy to run after birds, and birds use energy to fly.
Living creatures use food as energy so they can grow and move.
HOT DOGS
HOT DOGS
But we also use fuels for energy.
Gasoline powers motorcycles, cars, and trucks.
In fact, nothing happens without energy. Let's talk to a friend of mine who knows all about it.
DEPARTMENT OF ENERGY

ENERGY AND WORK

Scientists define energy as the ability to do work. Scientists also have a specific definition for work. Work is motion against resistance. For example, lifting a book up in the air against the pull of gravity is work.

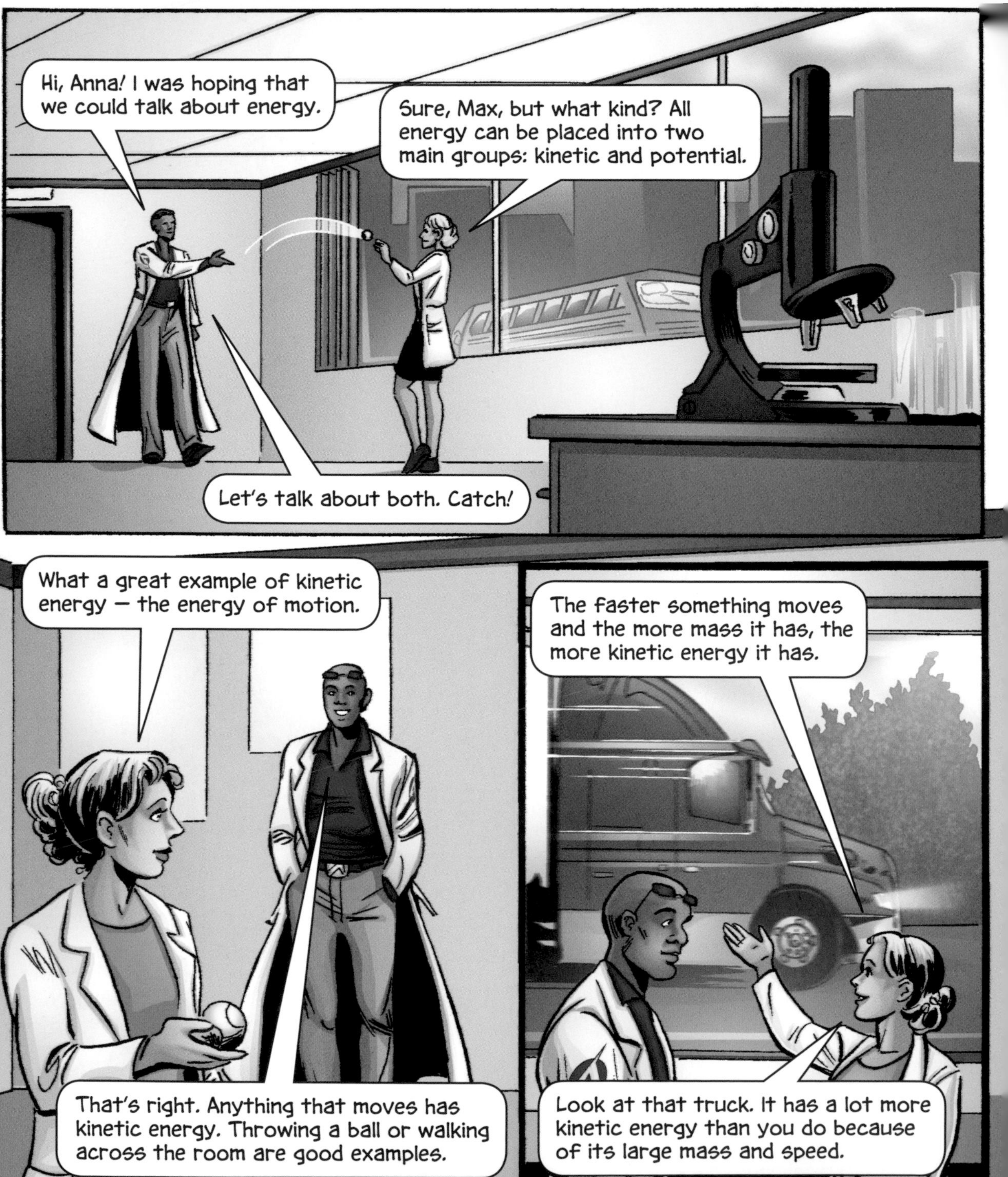
Hi, Anna! I was hoping that we could talk about energy.
Sure, Max, but what kind? All energy can be placed into two main groups: kinetic and potential.
Let's talk about both. Catch!
What a great example of kinetic energy — the energy of motion.
That's right. Anything that moves has kinetic energy. Throwing a ball or walking across the room are good examples.
The faster something moves and the more mass it has, the more kinetic energy it has.
Look at that truck. It has a lot more kinetic energy than you do because of its large mass and speed.

MASS AND MATTER

Mass is the amount of matter that makes up an object. Matter is something that takes up space. For example, a truck has more mass than a person does.

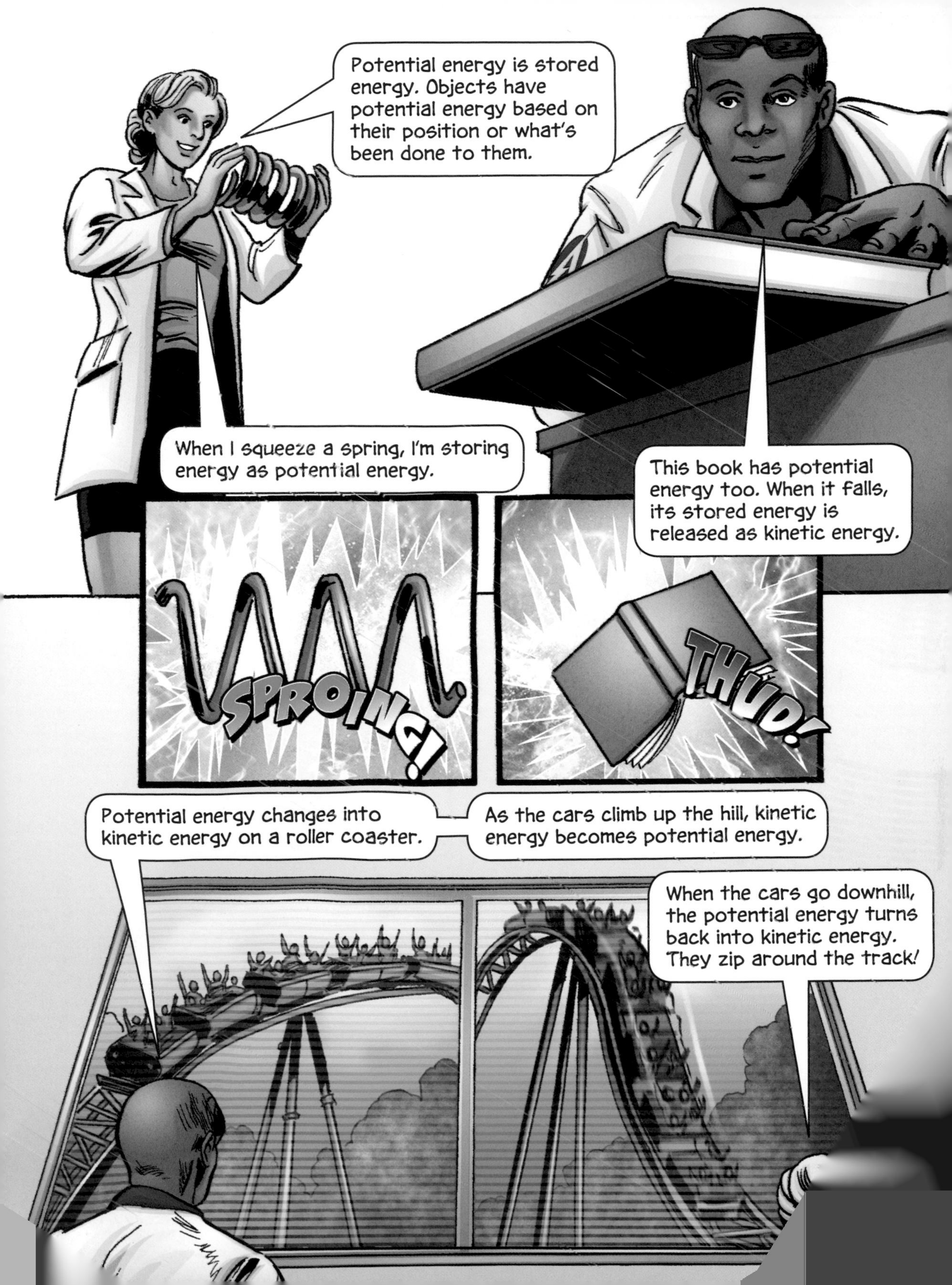
Potential energy is stored energy. Objects have potential energy based on their position or what's been done to them.
This book has potential energy too. When it falls, its stored energy is released as kinetic energy.
When I squeeze a spring, I'm storing energy as potential energy.
SPROING!
THUD!
Potential energy changes into kinetic energy on a roller coaster.
As the cars climb up the hill, kinetic energy becomes potential energy.
When the cars go downhill, the potential energy turns back into kinetic energy. They zip around the track!

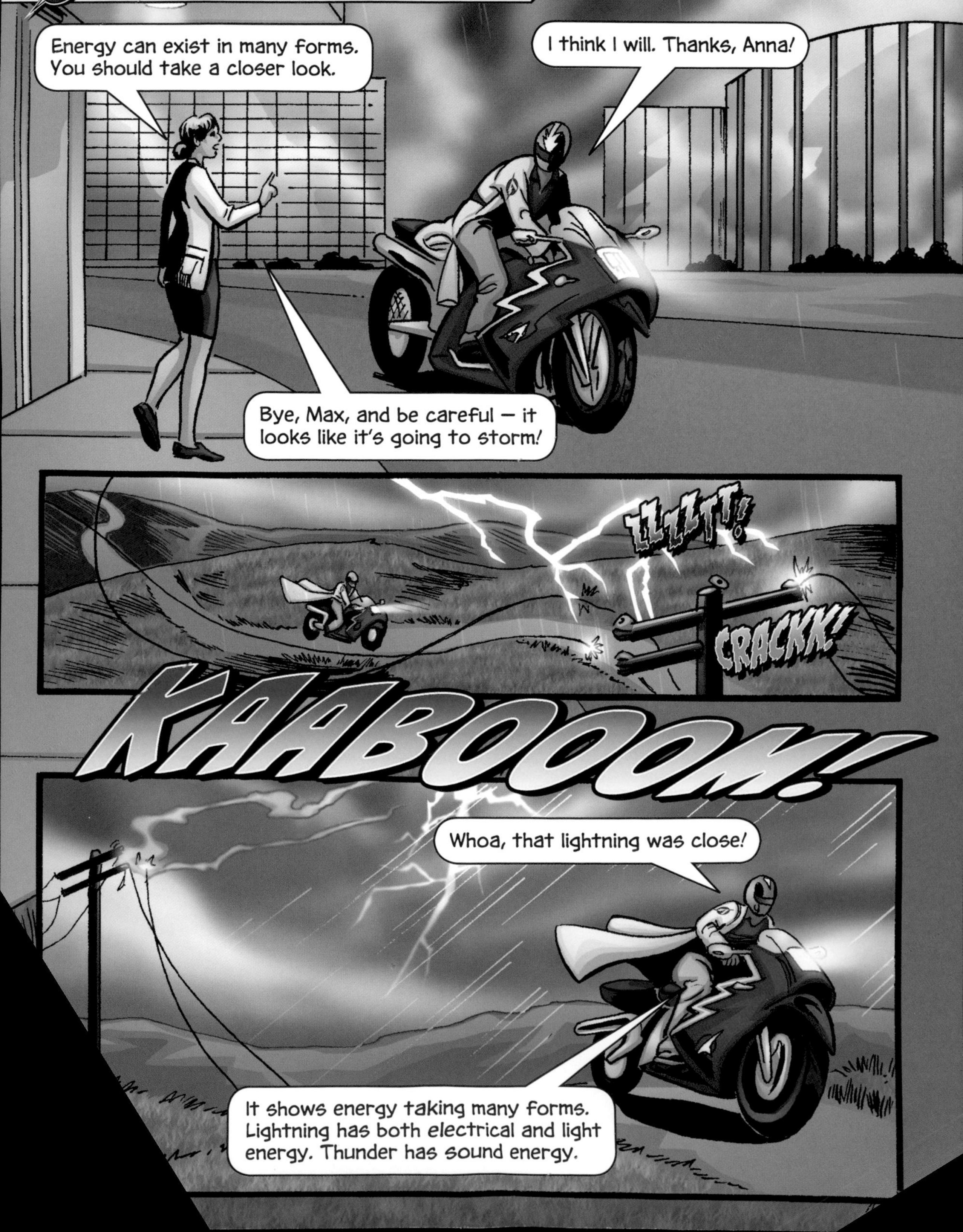
Energy can exist in many forms. You should take a closer look.
I think I will. Thanks, Anna!
Bye, Max, and be careful — it looks like it's going to storm!
ZZZZTT!
CRACKK!
KAABOOOM!
Whoa, that lightning was close!
It shows energy taking many forms. Lightning has both electrical and light energy. Thunder has sound energy.

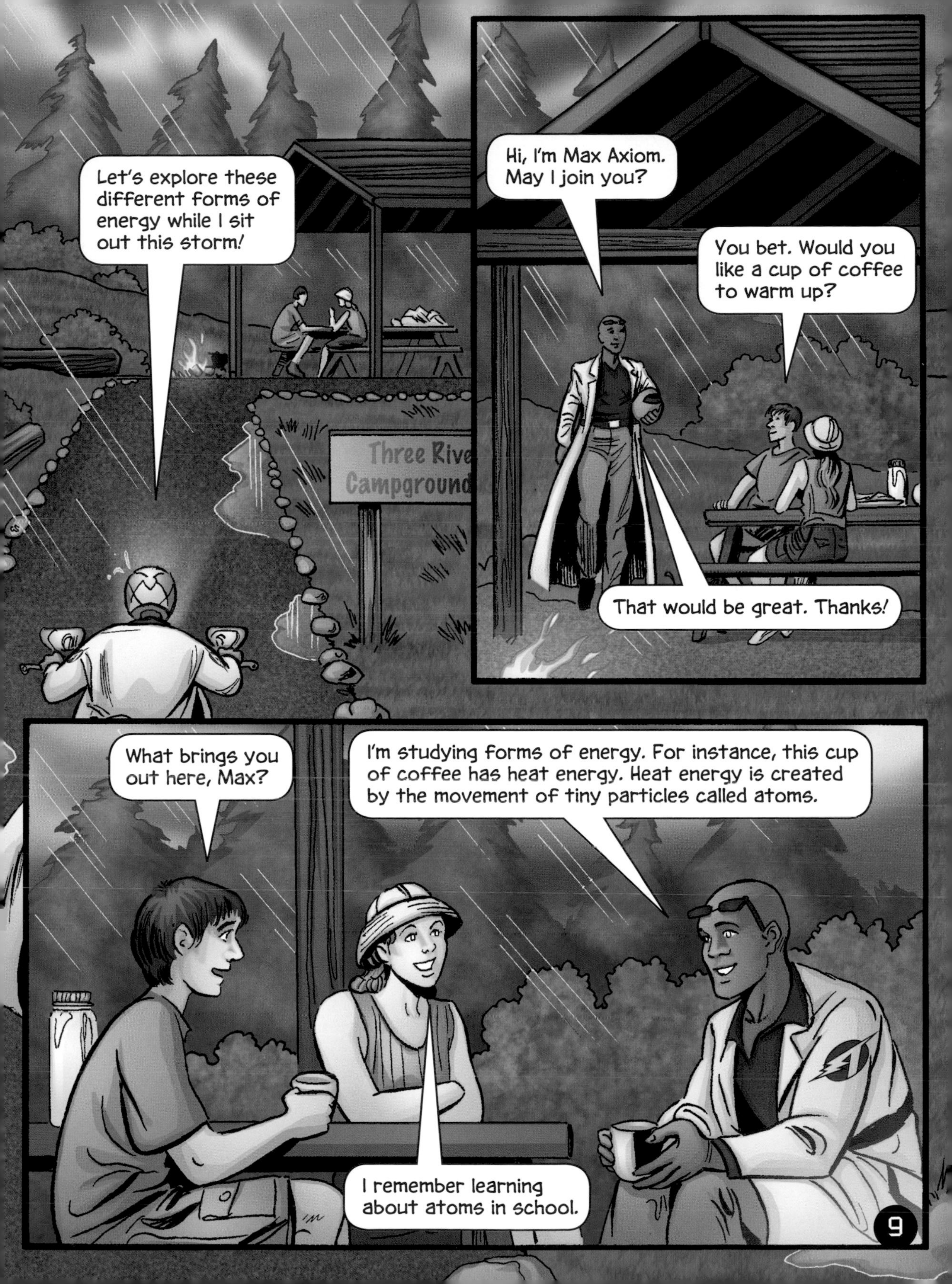

Let's explore these different forms of energy while I sit out this storm!
Three Rive
Campground
Hi, I'm Max Axiom. May I join you?
You bet. Would you like a cup of coffee to warm up?
That would be great. Thanks!
What brings you out here, Max?
I'm studying forms of energy. For instance, this cup of coffee has heat energy. Heat energy is created by the movement of tiny particles called atoms.
I remember learning about atoms in school.

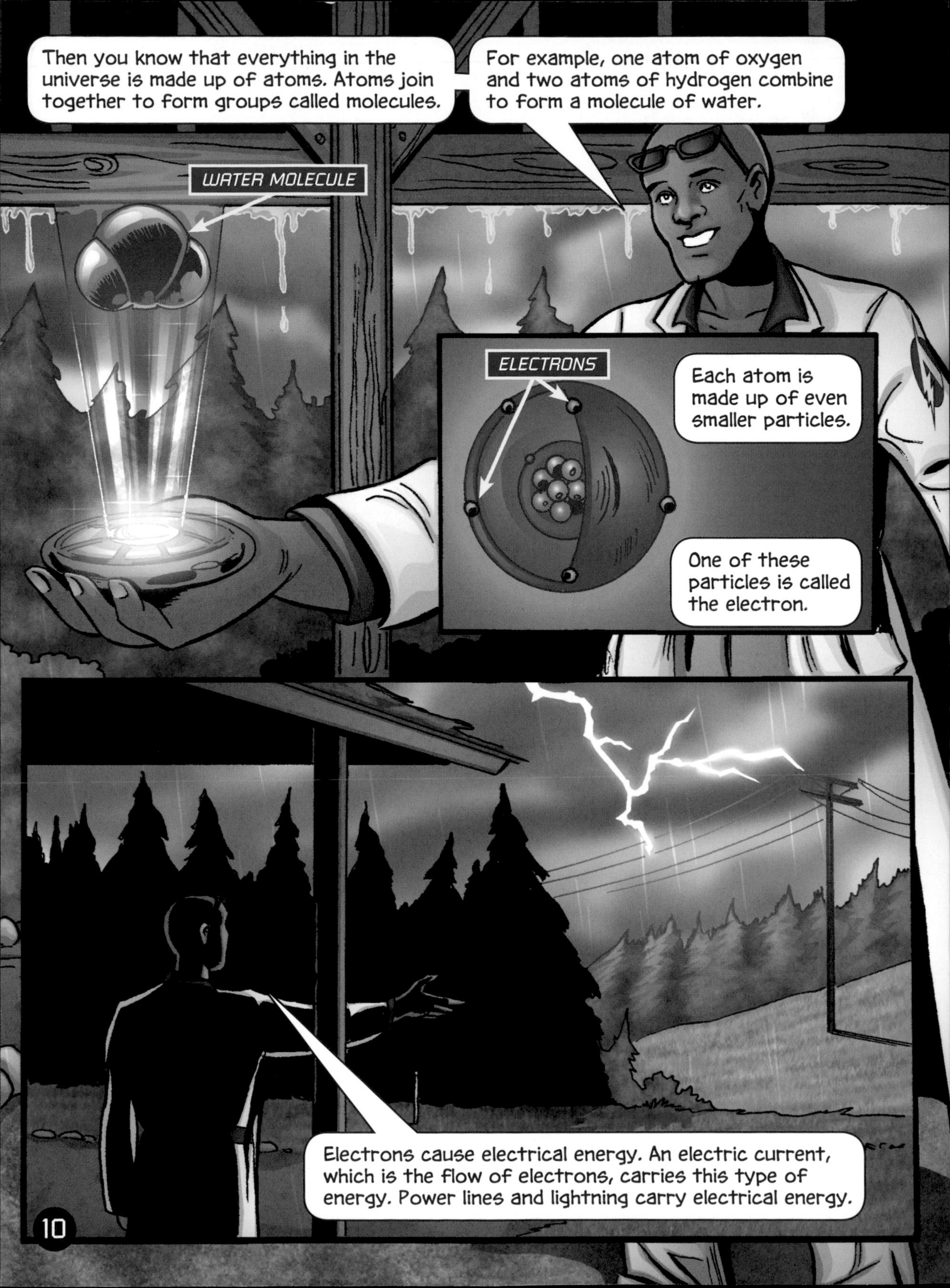

Then you know that everything in the universe is made up of atoms. Atoms join together to form groups called molecules.
For example, one atom of oxygen and two atoms of hydrogen combine to form a molecule of water.
WATER MOLECULE
ELECTRONS
Each atom is made up of even smaller particles.
One of these particles is called the electron.
Electrons cause electrical energy. An electric current, which is the flow of electrons, carries this type of energy. Power lines and lightning carry electrical energy.

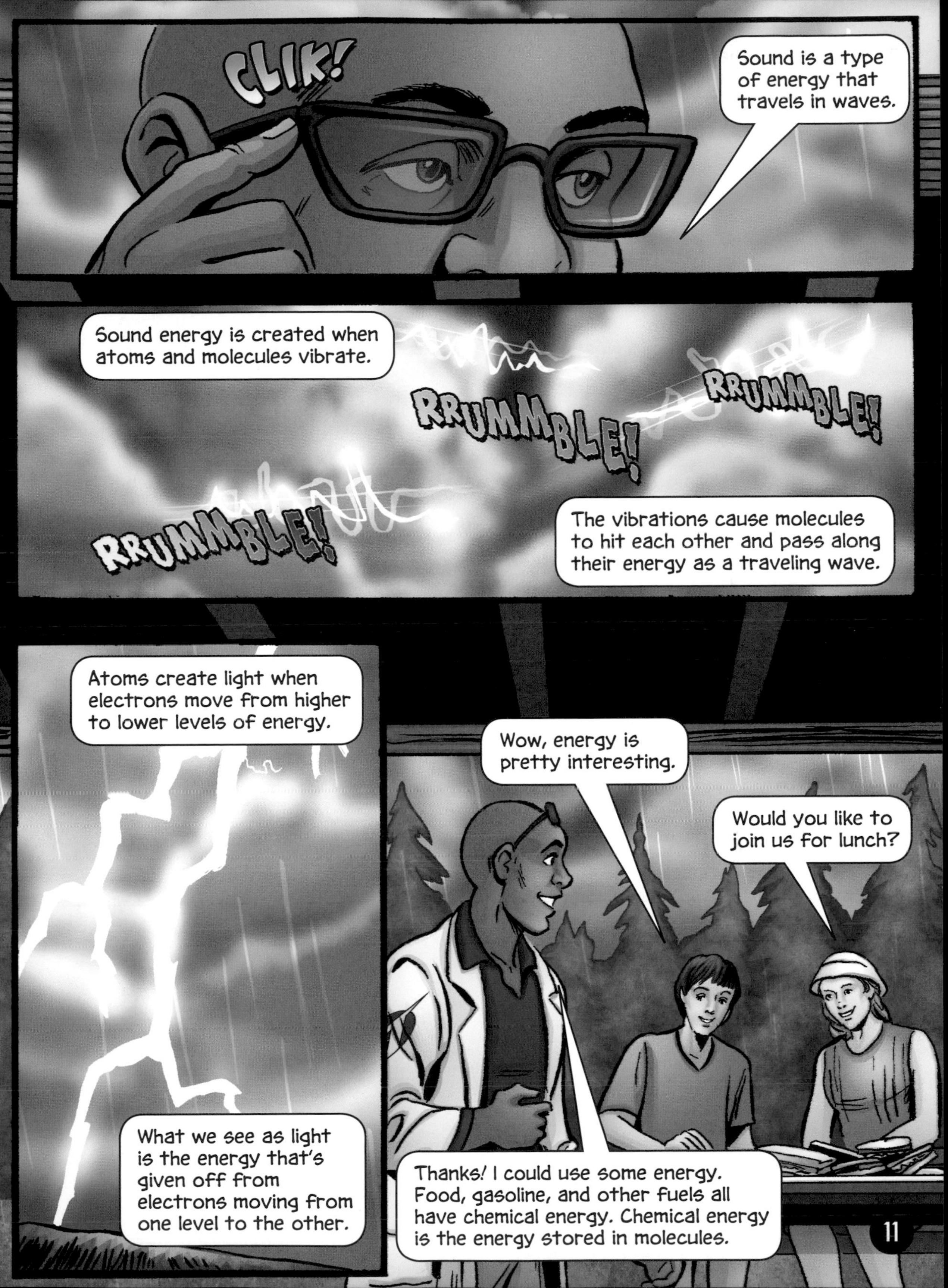
CLIK!
Sound is a type of energy that travels in waves.
Sound energy is created when atoms and molecules vibrate.
RRUMMBLE!
RRUMMBLE!
RRUMMBLE!
The vibrations cause molecules to hit each other and pass along their energy as a traveling wave.
Atoms create light when electrons move from higher to lower levels of energy.
What we see as light is the energy that's given off from electrons moving from one level to the other.
Wow, energy is pretty interesting.
Would you like to join us for lunch?
Thanks! I could use some energy. Food, gasoline, and other fuels all have chemical energy. Chemical energy is the energy stored in molecules.

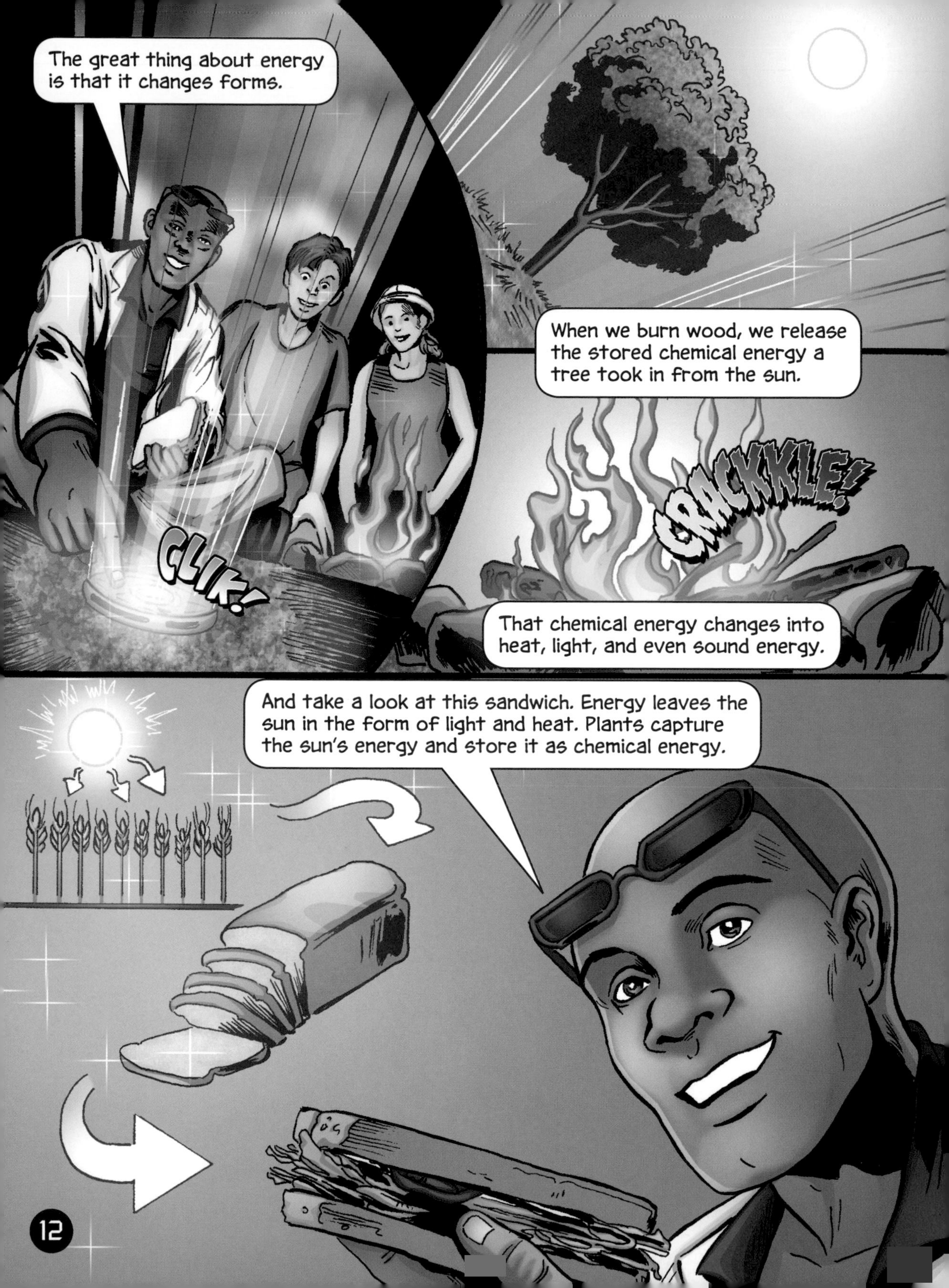

The great thing about energy is that it changes forms.
CLIK!
When we burn wood, we release the stored chemical energy a tree took in from the sun.
CRACKKLE!
That chemical energy changes into heat, light, and even sound energy.
And take a look at this sandwich. Energy leaves the sun in the form of light and heat. Plants capture the sun's energy and store it as chemical energy.

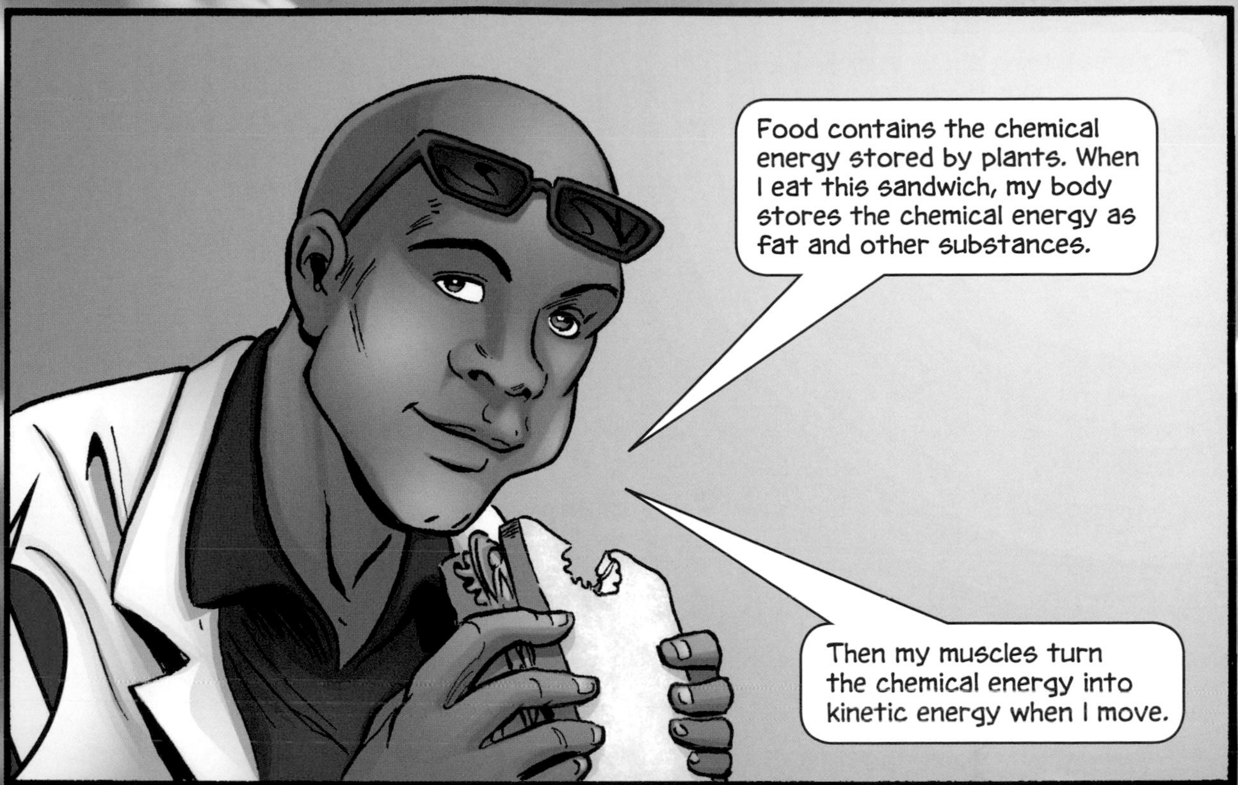
Food contains the chemical energy stored by plants. When I eat this sandwich, my body stores the chemical energy as fat and other substances.
Then my muscles turn the chemical energy into kinetic energy when I move.

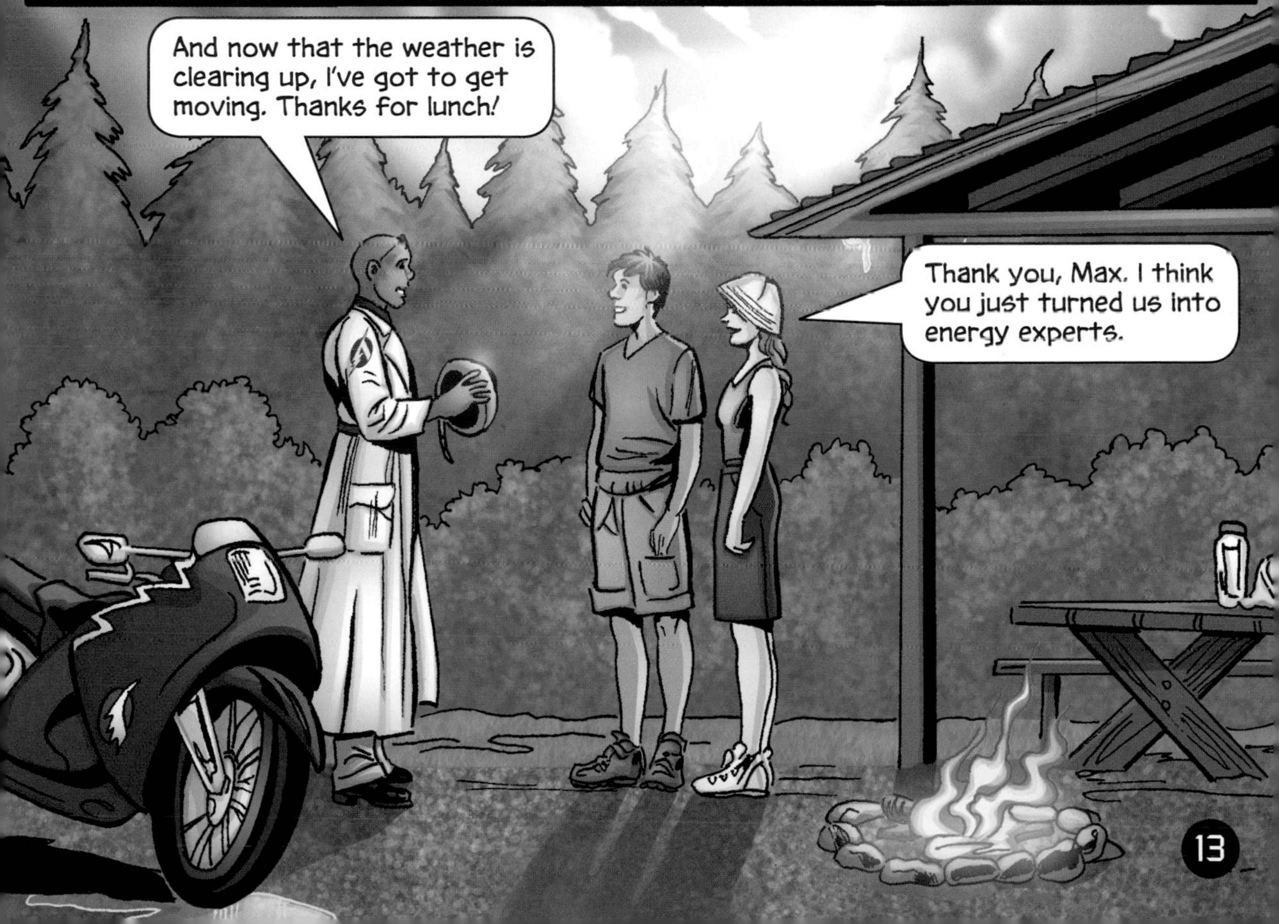
And now that the weather is clearing up, I've got to get moving. Thanks for lunch!
Thank you, Max. I think you just turned us into energy experts.

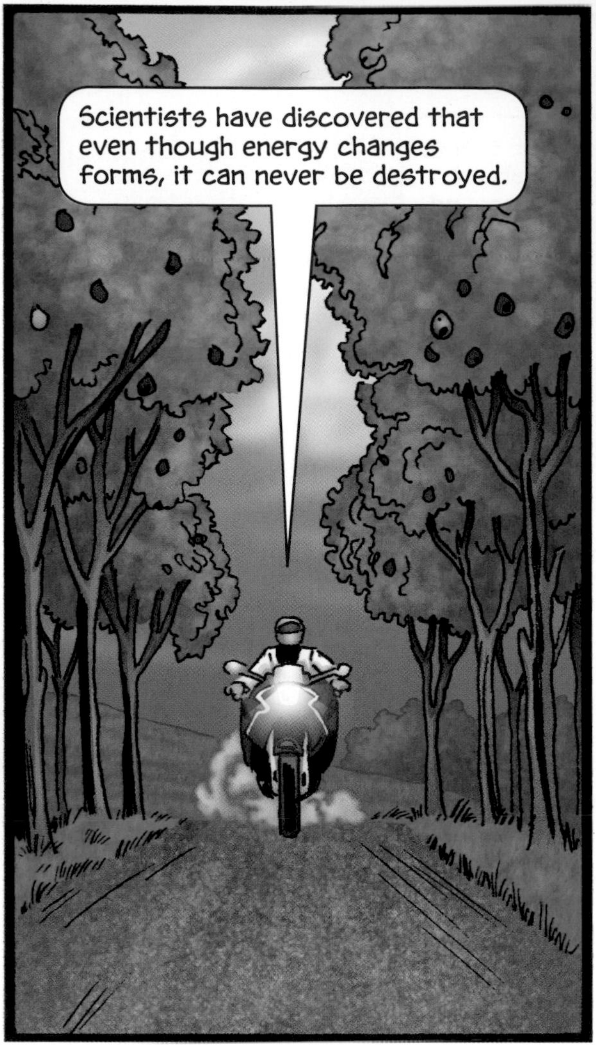
Scientists have discovered that even though energy changes forms, it can never be destroyed.

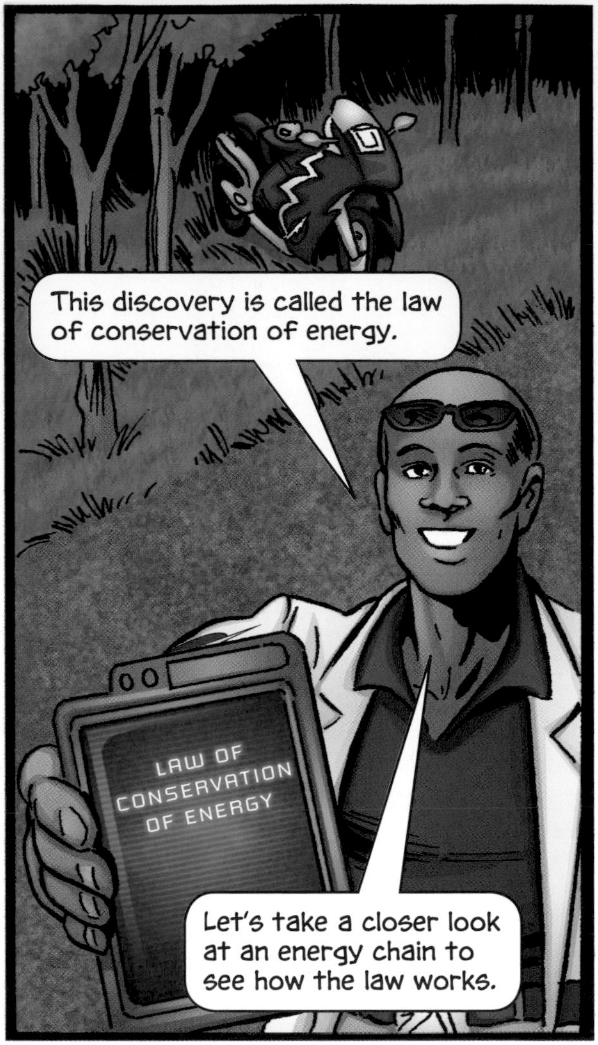
This discovery is called the law of conservation of energy.
LAW OF CONSERVATION OF ENERGY
Let's take a closer look at an energy chain to see how the law works.

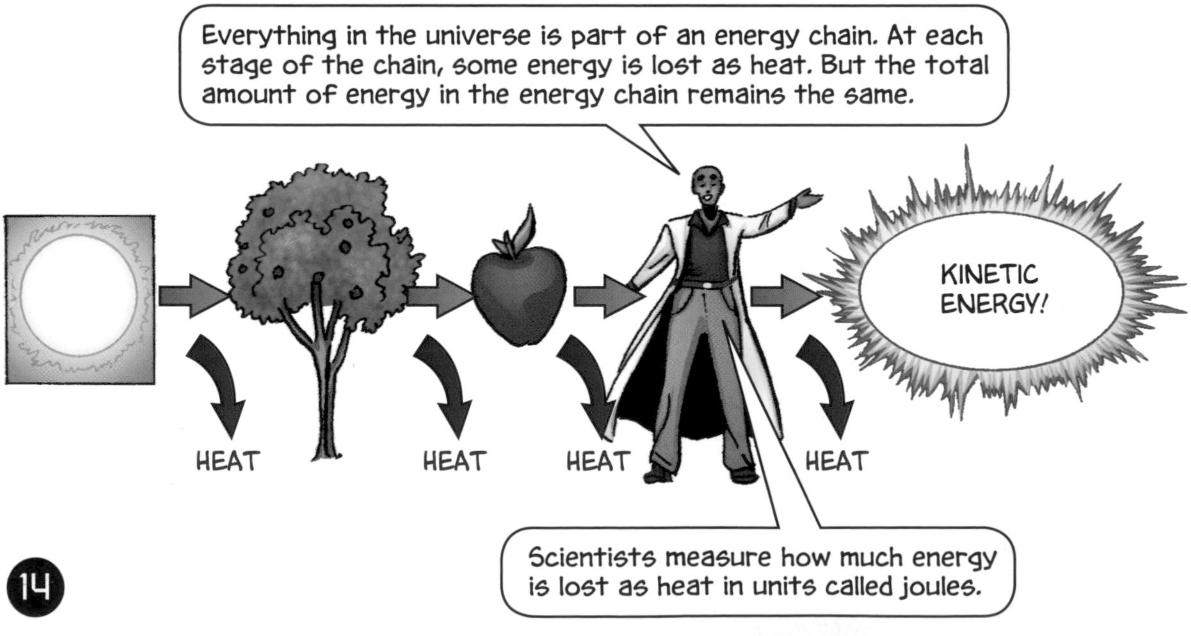
Everything in the universe is part of an energy chain. At each stage of the chain, some energy is lost as heat. But the total amount of energy in the energy chain remains the same.
KINETIC ENERGY!
HEAT
HEAT
HEAT
HEAT
Scientists measure how much energy is lost as heat in units called joules.

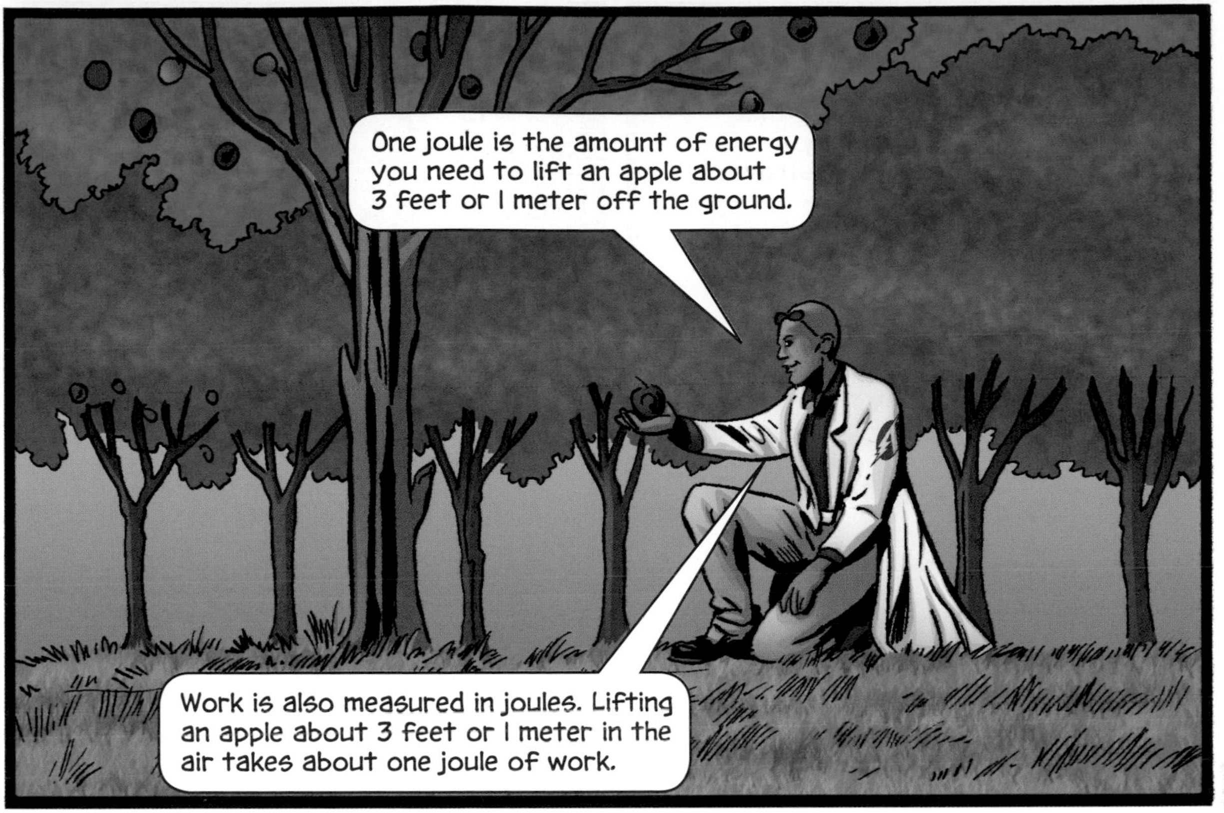
One joule is the amount of energy you need to lift an apple about 3 feet or 1 meter off the ground.
Work is also measured in joules. Lifting an apple about 3 feet or 1 meter in the air takes about one joule of work.

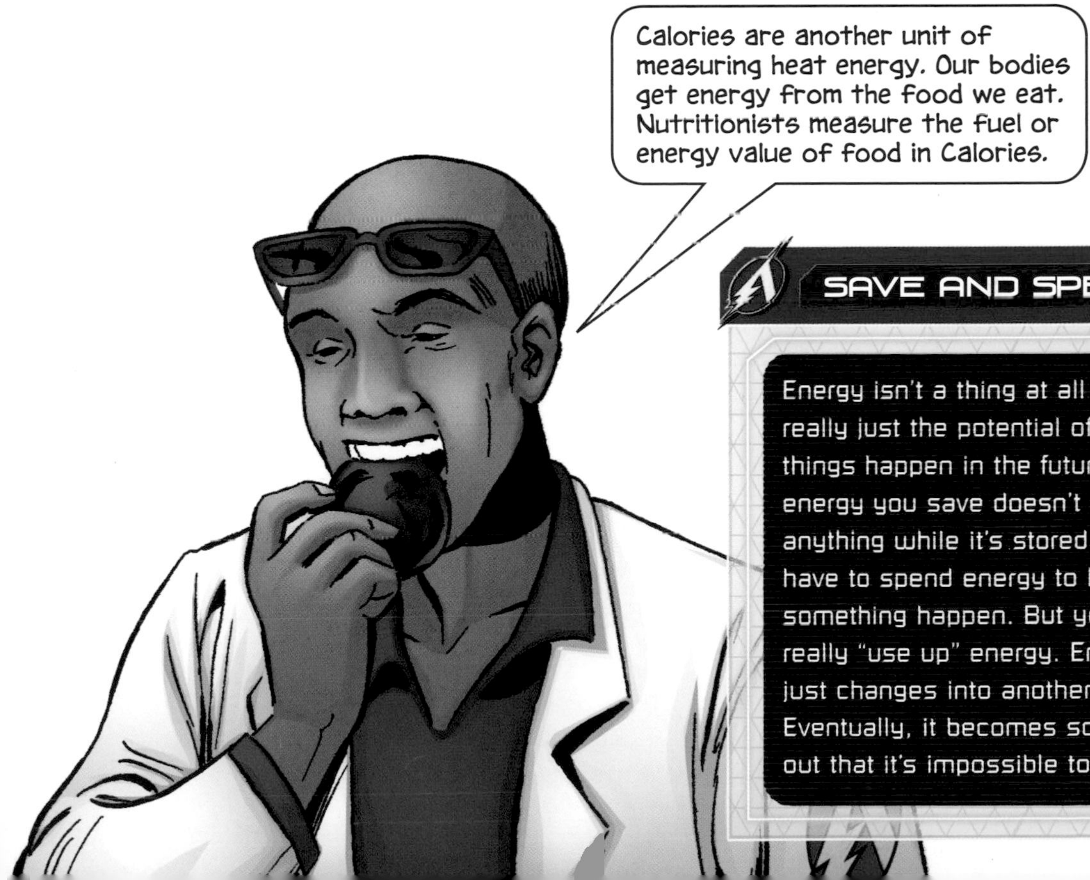
Calories are another unit of measuring heat energy. Our bodies get energy from the food we eat. Nutritionists measure the fuel or energy value of food in Calories.

SAVE AND SPEND

Energy isn't a thing at all — it's really just the potential of making things happen in the future. The energy you save doesn't do anything while it's stored. You have to spend energy to have something happen. But you never really "use up" energy. Energy just changes into another form. Eventually, it becomes so spread out that it's impossible to use.

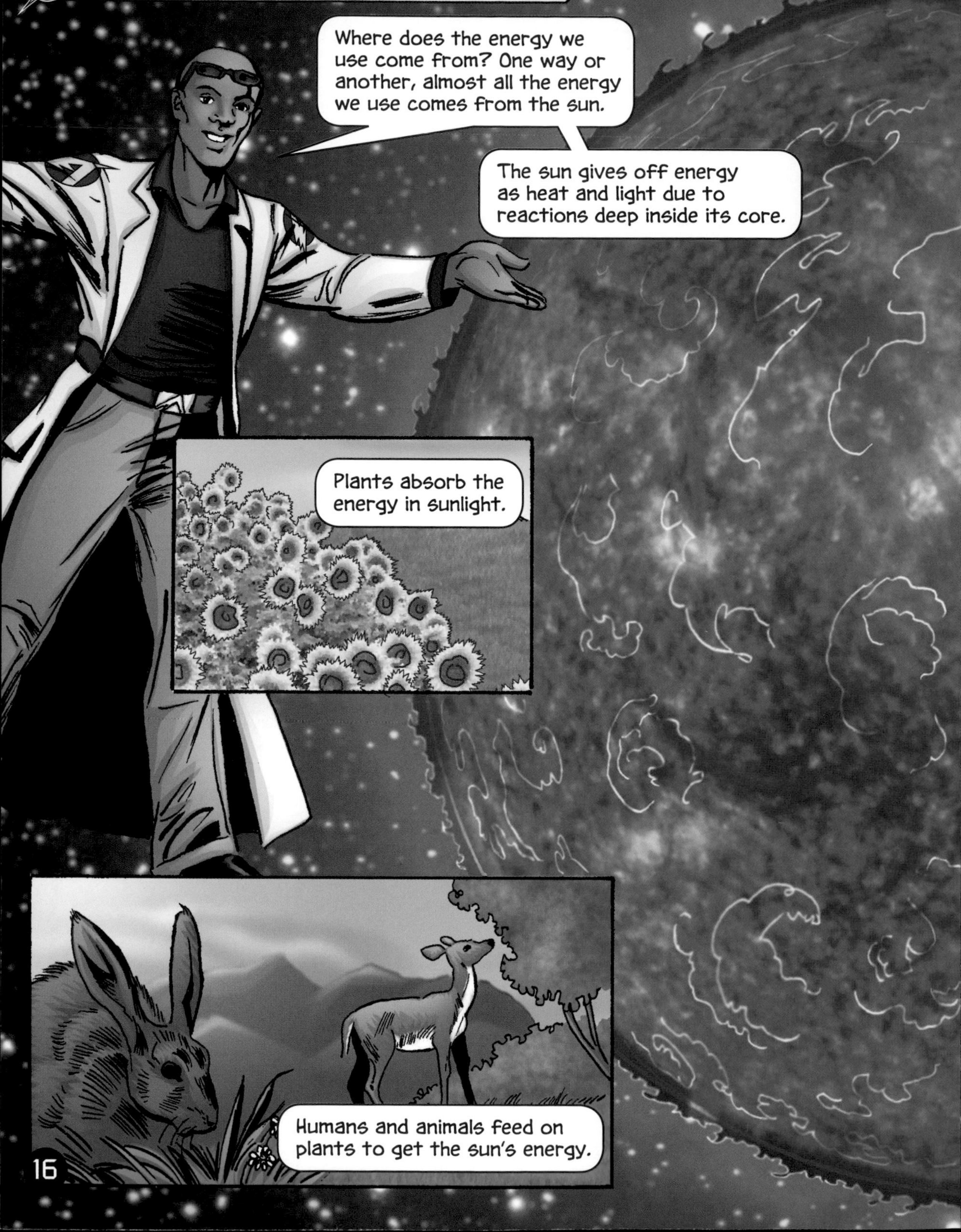
Where does the energy we use come from? One way or another, almost all the energy we use comes from the sun.
The sun gives off energy as heat and light due to reactions deep inside its core.
Plants absorb the energy in sunlight.
Humans and animals feed on plants to get the sun's energy.

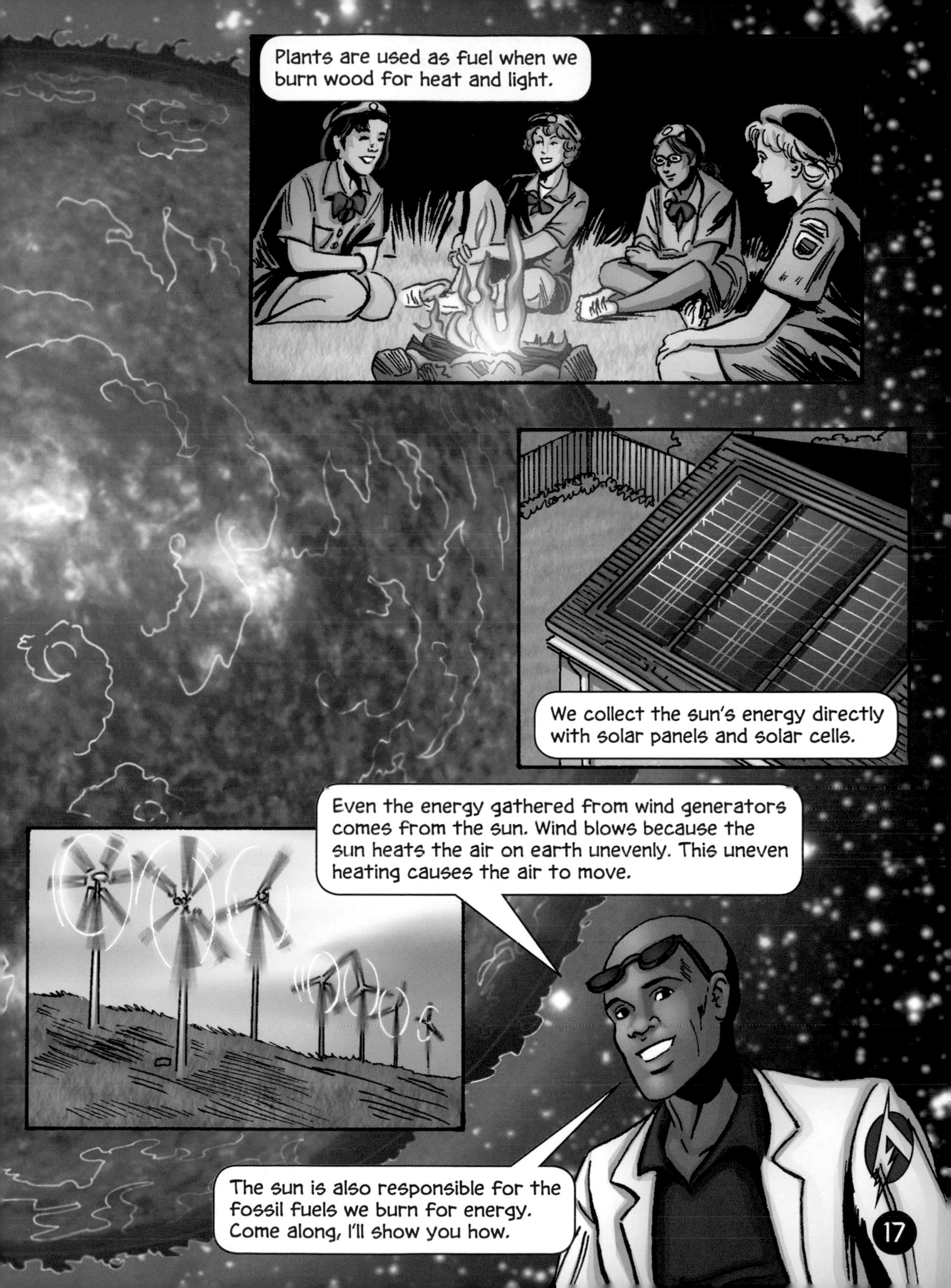

Plants are used as fuel when we burn wood for heat and light.
We collect the sun's energy directly with solar panels and solar cells.
Even the energy gathered from wind generators comes from the sun. Wind blows because the sun heats the air on earth unevenly. This uneven heating causes the air to move.
The sun is also responsible for the fossil fuels we burn for energy. Come along, I'll show you how.

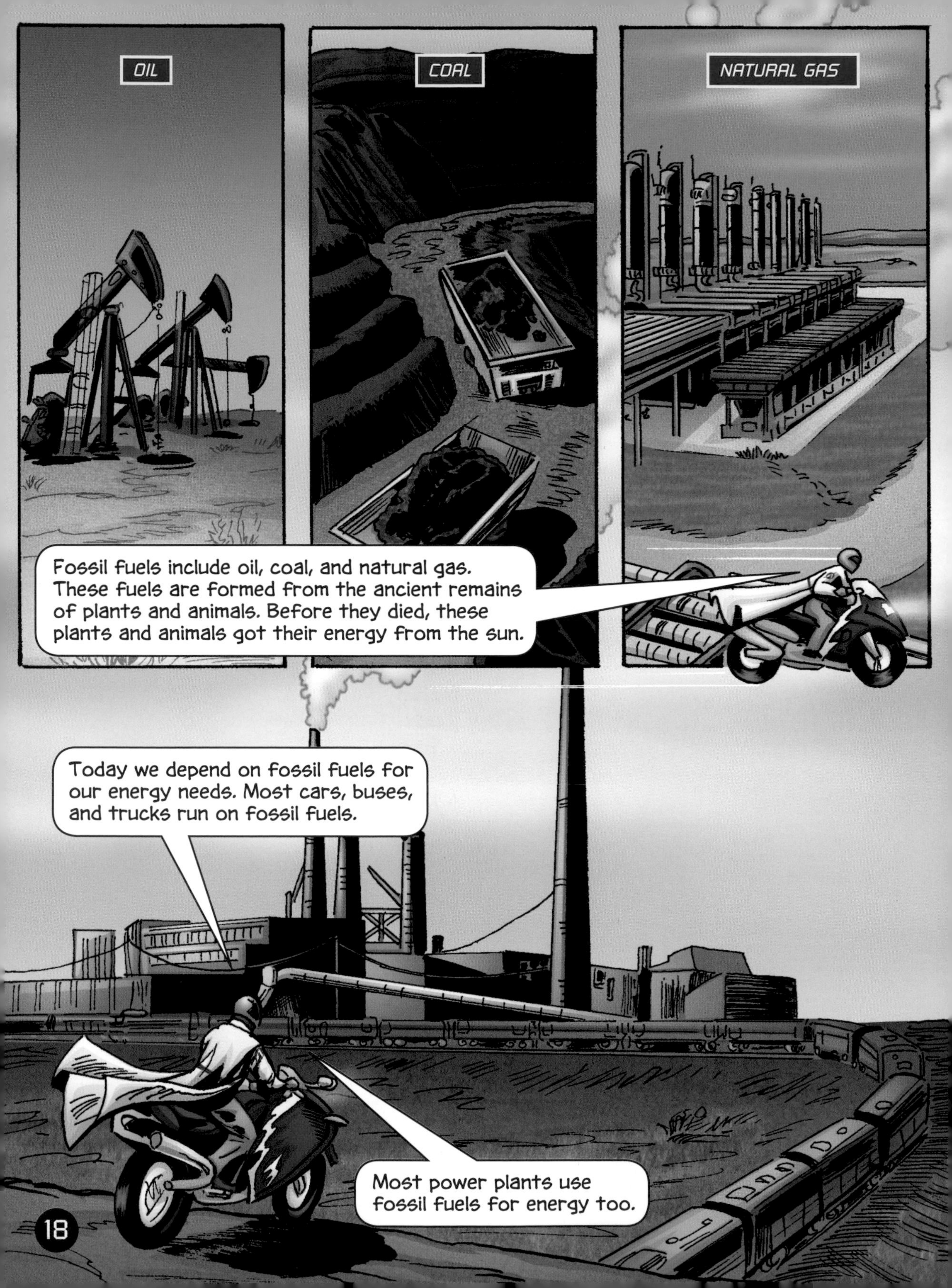
OIL
COAL
NATURAL GAS
Fossil fuels include oil, coal, and natural gas. These fuels are formed from the ancient remains of plants and animals. Before they died, these plants and animals got their energy from the sun.
Today we depend on fossil fuels for our energy needs. Most cars, buses, and trucks run on fossil fuels.
Most power plants use fossil fuels for energy too.

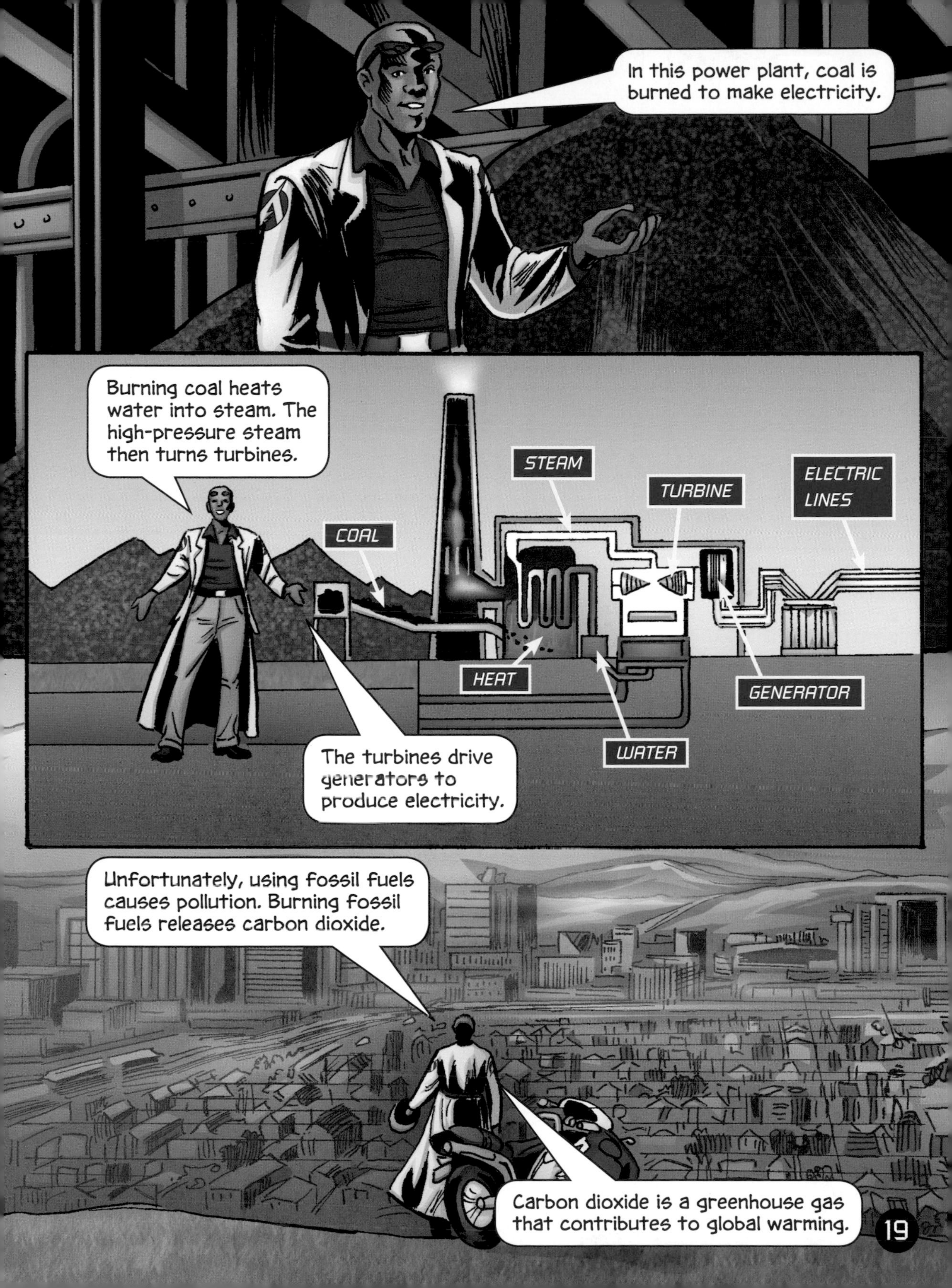

In this power plant, coal is burned to make electricity.
Burning coal heats water into steam. The high-pressure steam then turns turbines.
STEAM
TURBINE
ELECTRIC LINES
COAL
HEAT
GENERATOR
WATER
The turbines drive generators to produce electricity.
Unfortunately, using fossil fuels causes pollution. Burning fossil fuels releases carbon dioxide.
Carbon dioxide is a greenhouse gas that contributes to global warming.

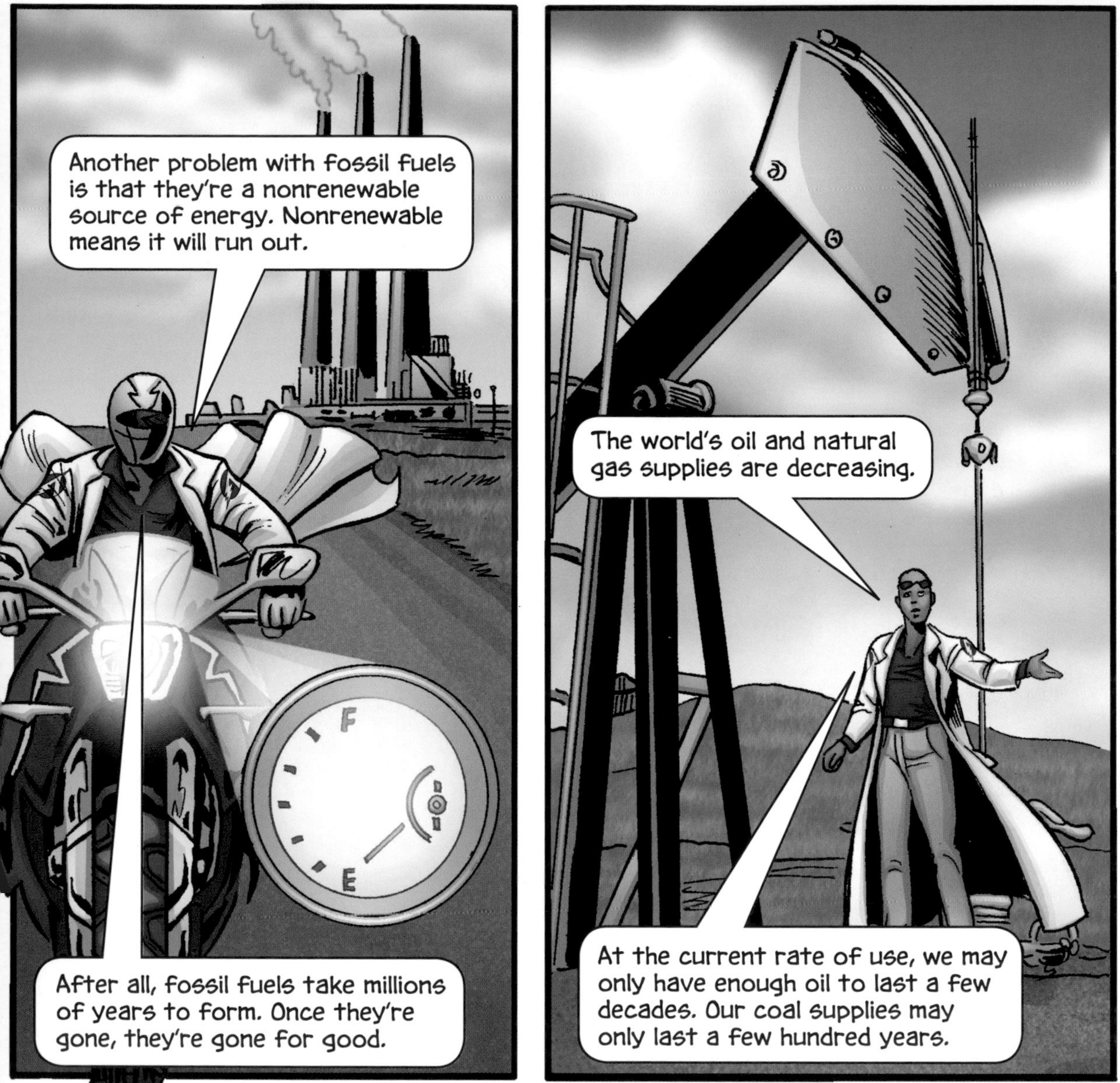
Another problem with fossil fuels is that they're a nonrenewable source of energy. Nonrenewable means it will run out.
After all, fossil fuels take millions of years to form. Once they're gone, they're gone for good.
F
E
The world's oil and natural gas supplies are decreasing.
At the current rate of use, we may only have enough oil to last a few decades. Our coal supplies may only last a few hundred years.

BURNING OIL

ACCESS GRANTED: MAX AXIOM

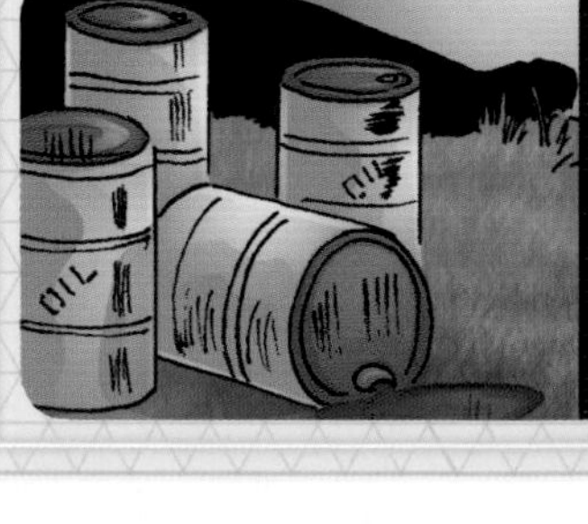

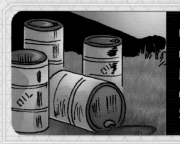

Oil is one of the most important sources of energy in the world. Refineries make oil into gasoline for our cars and jet fuel for our planes. Oil is even used in products such as crayons, tires, and dishwashing liquid. In fact, the United States uses about 20 million barrels of oil every day.

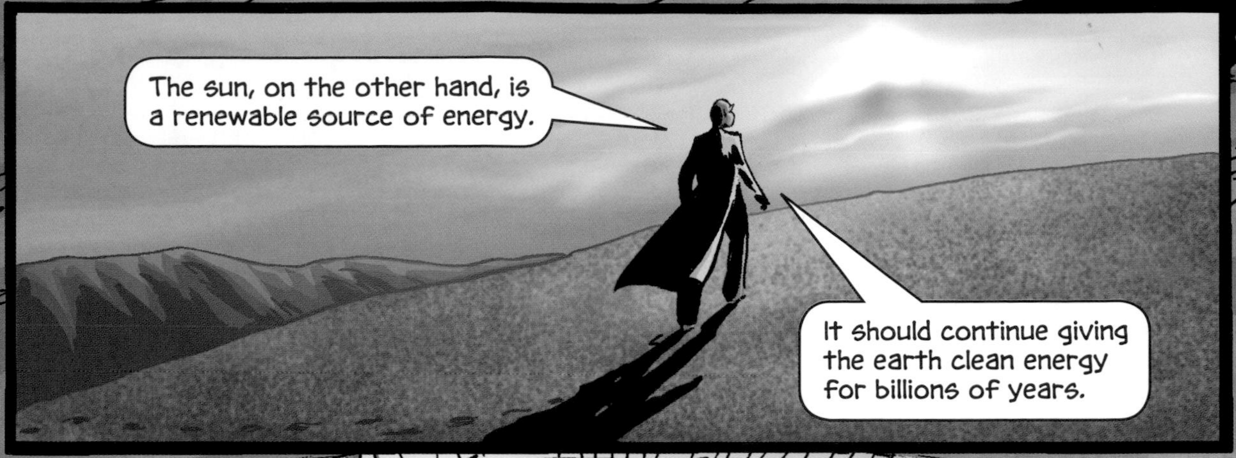
The sun, on the other hand, is a renewable source of energy.
It should continue giving the earth clean energy for billions of years.

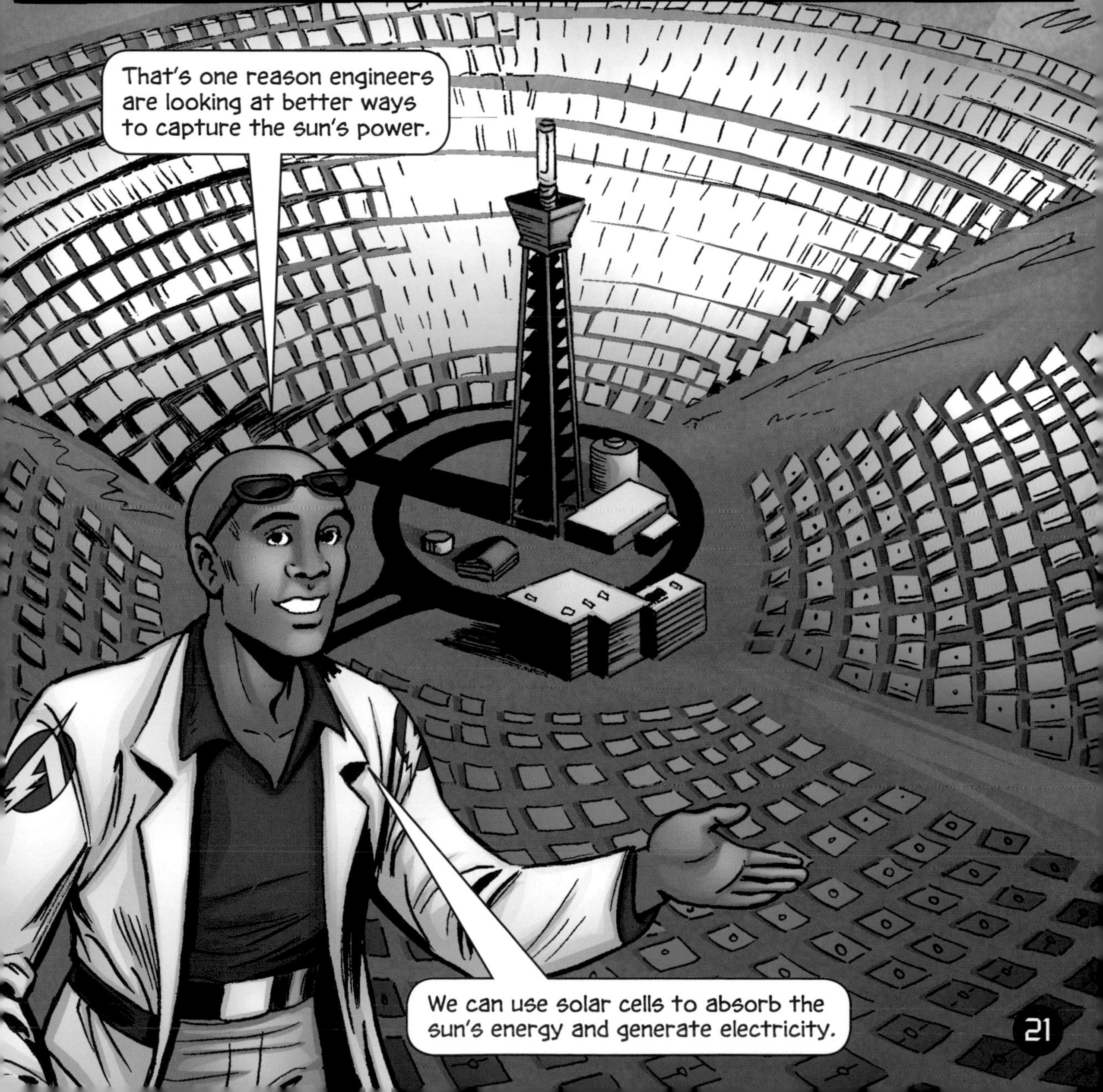
That's one reason engineers are looking at better ways to capture the sun's power.
We can use solar cells to absorb the sun's energy and generate electricity.

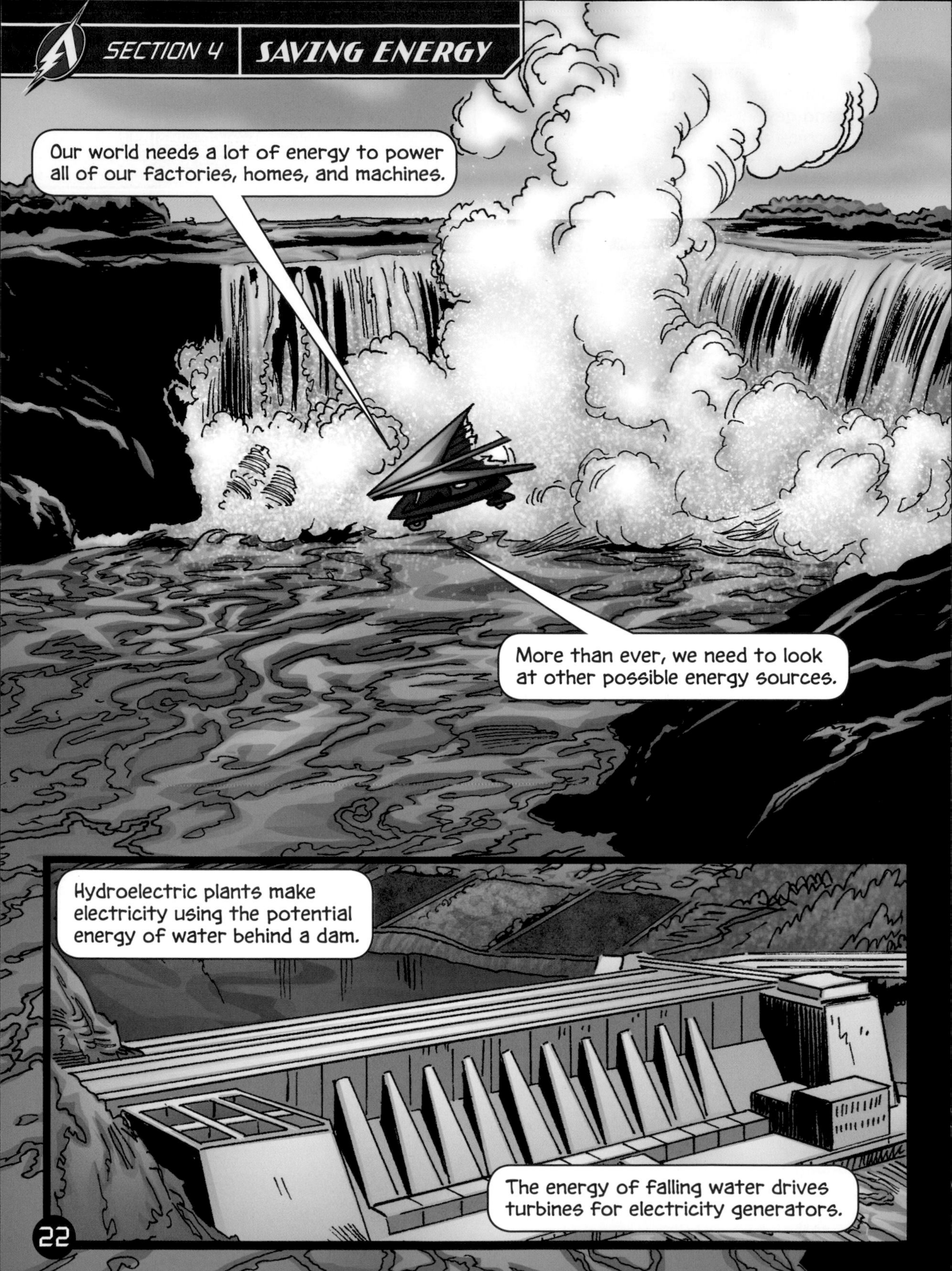
Our world needs a lot of energy to power all of our factories, homes, and machines.
More than ever, we need to look at other possible energy sources.
Hydroelectric plants make electricity using the potential energy of water behind a dam.
The energy of falling water drives turbines for electricity generators.

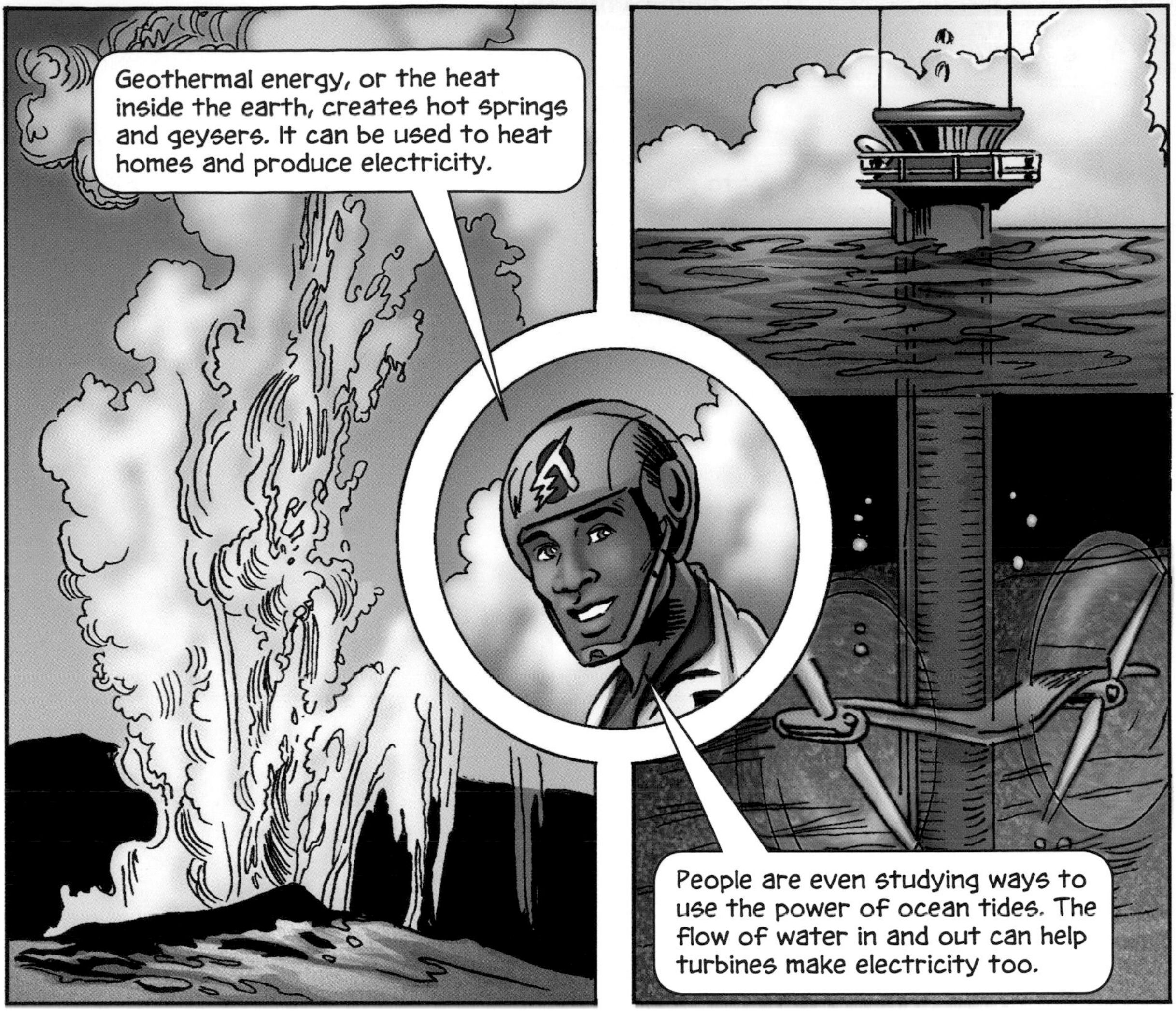
Geothermal energy, or the heat inside the earth, creates hot springs and geysers. It can be used to heat homes and produce electricity.
People are even studying ways to use the power of ocean tides. The flow of water in and out can help turbines make electricity too.

NUCLEAR POWER

ACCESS GRANTED: MAX AXIOM

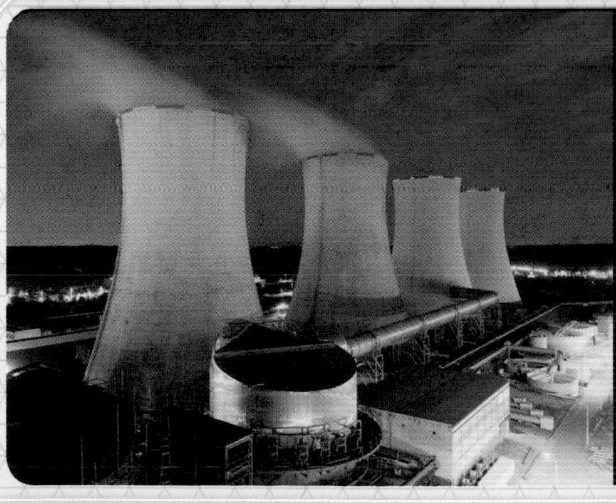

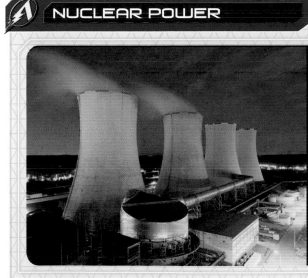

In nuclear power plants, a nuclear reactor splits atoms to generate heat. This heat turns water into steam. The steam drives turbines to produce electricity. Although nuclear power plants don't create pollutants like carbon dioxide, they do generate radioactive waste. Radiation from this waste has harmful long-term effects on people's health and the environment.

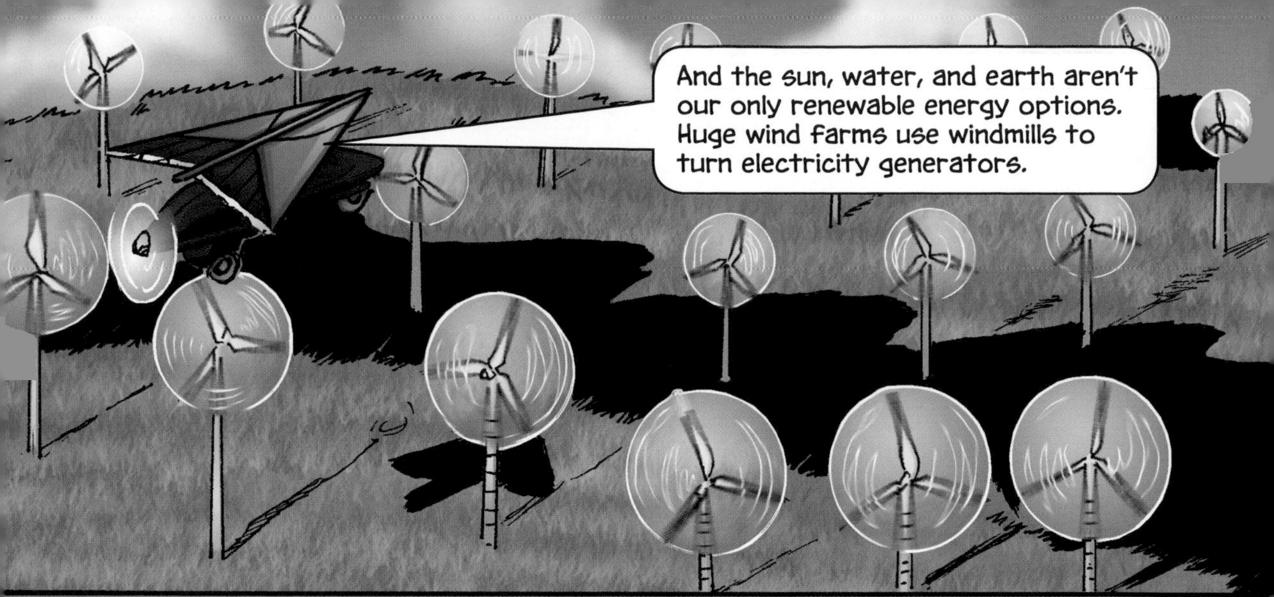
And the sun, water, and earth aren't our only renewable energy options. Huge wind farms use windmills to turn electricity generators.

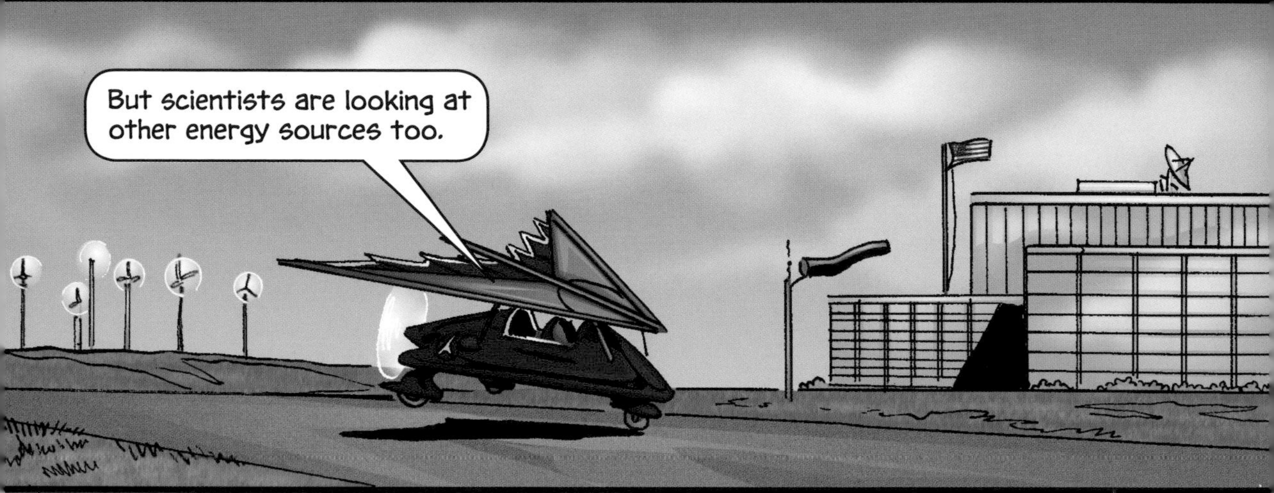
But scientists are looking at other energy sources too.

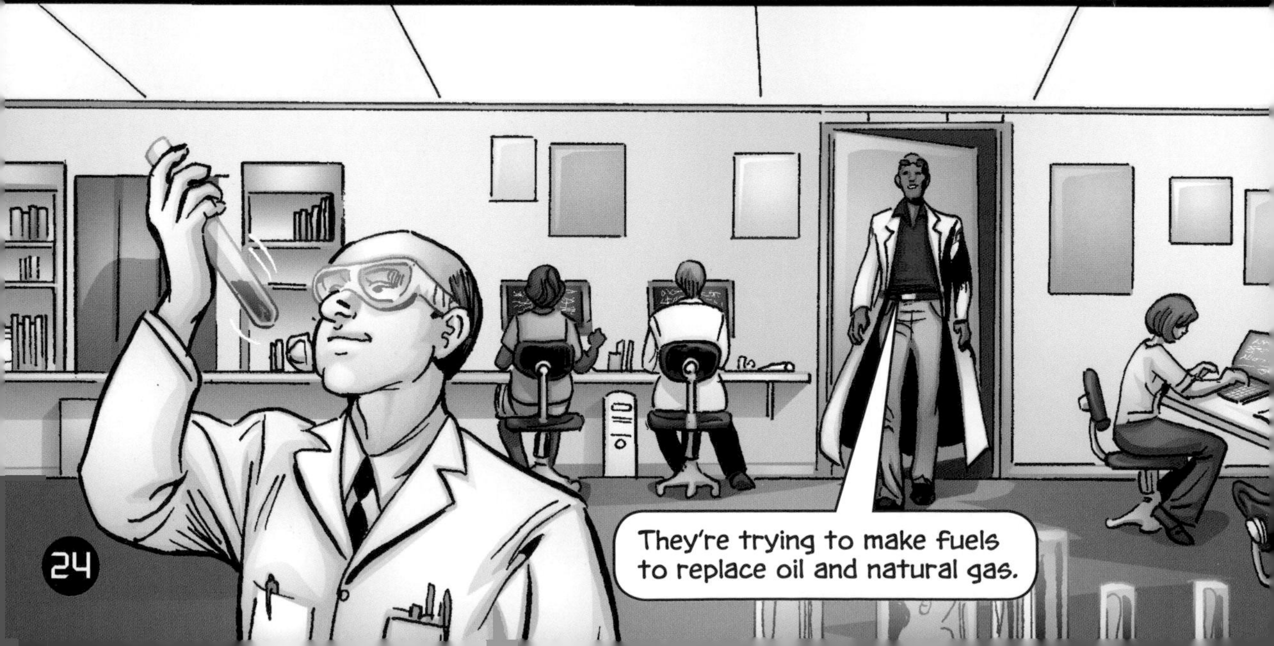
They're trying to make fuels to replace oil and natural gas.

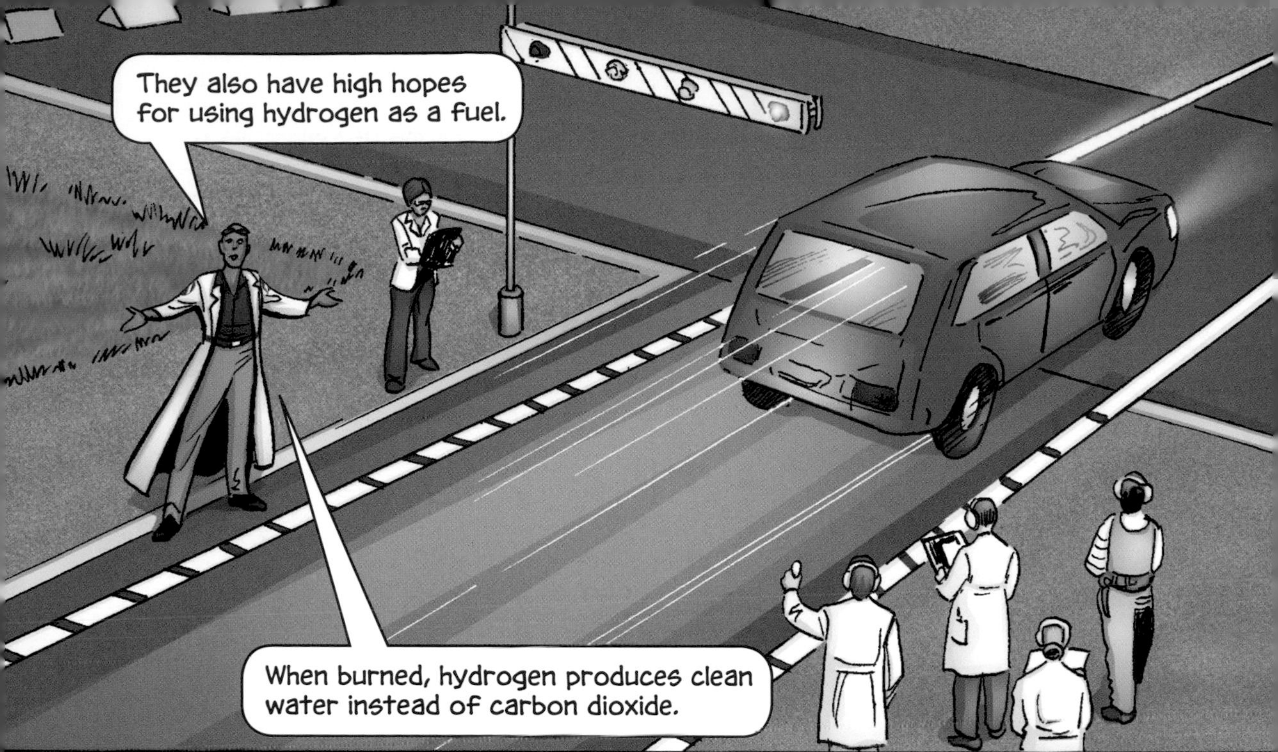
They also have high hopes for using hydrogen as a fuel.
When burned, hydrogen produces clean water instead of carbon dioxide.

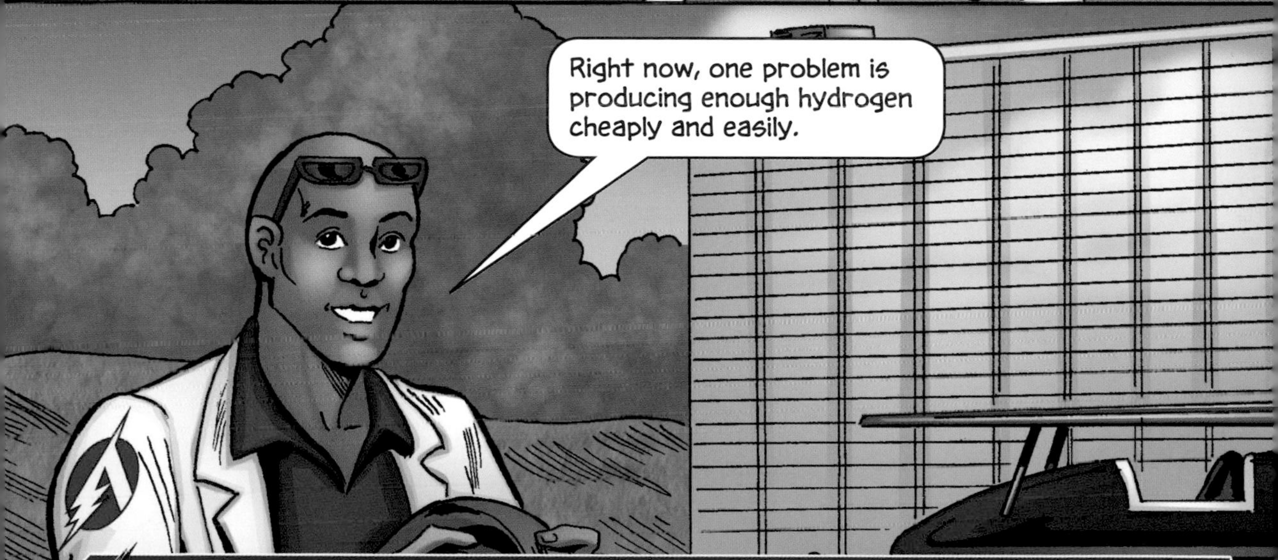
Right now, one problem is producing enough hydrogen cheaply and easily.

ETHANOL

ACCESS GRANTED: MAX AXIOM

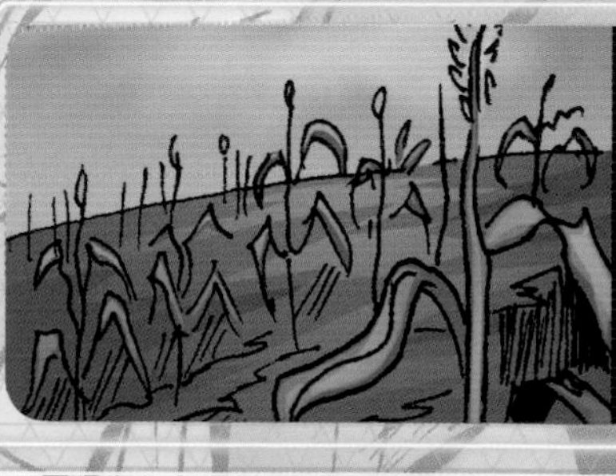

Ethanol is a renewable fuel made from plants such as corn and switch grass. Ethanol is used as an additive in gasoline. It is gaining popularity as an alternative fuel for vehicles. Researchers are trying to develop cost-effective and environmentally-friendly ways to use plants as fuels.

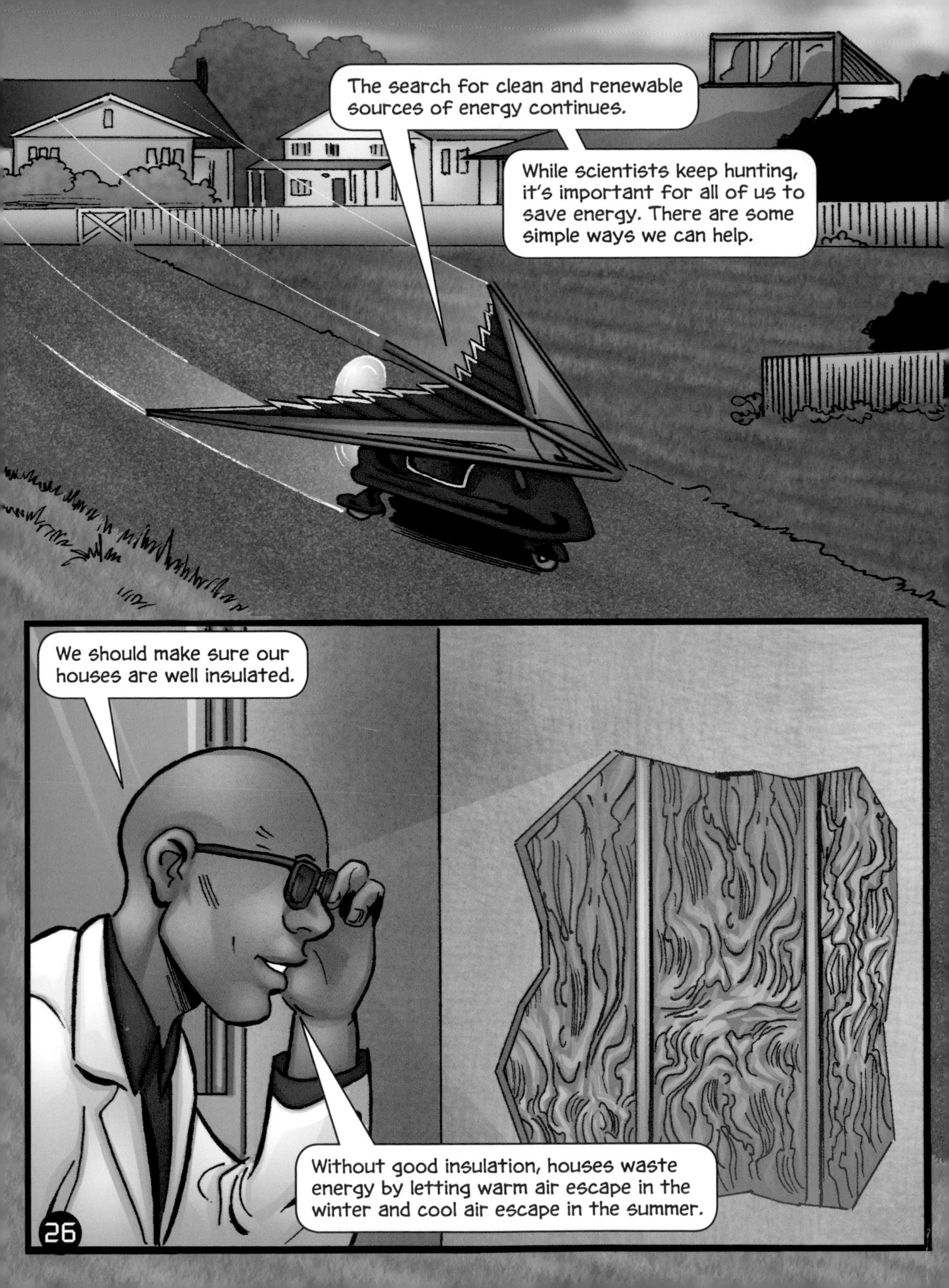
The search for clean and renewable sources of energy continues.
While scientists keep hunting, it's important for all of us to save energy. There are some simple ways we can help.
We should make sure our houses are well insulated.
Without good insulation, houses waste energy by letting warm air escape in the winter and cool air escape in the summer.

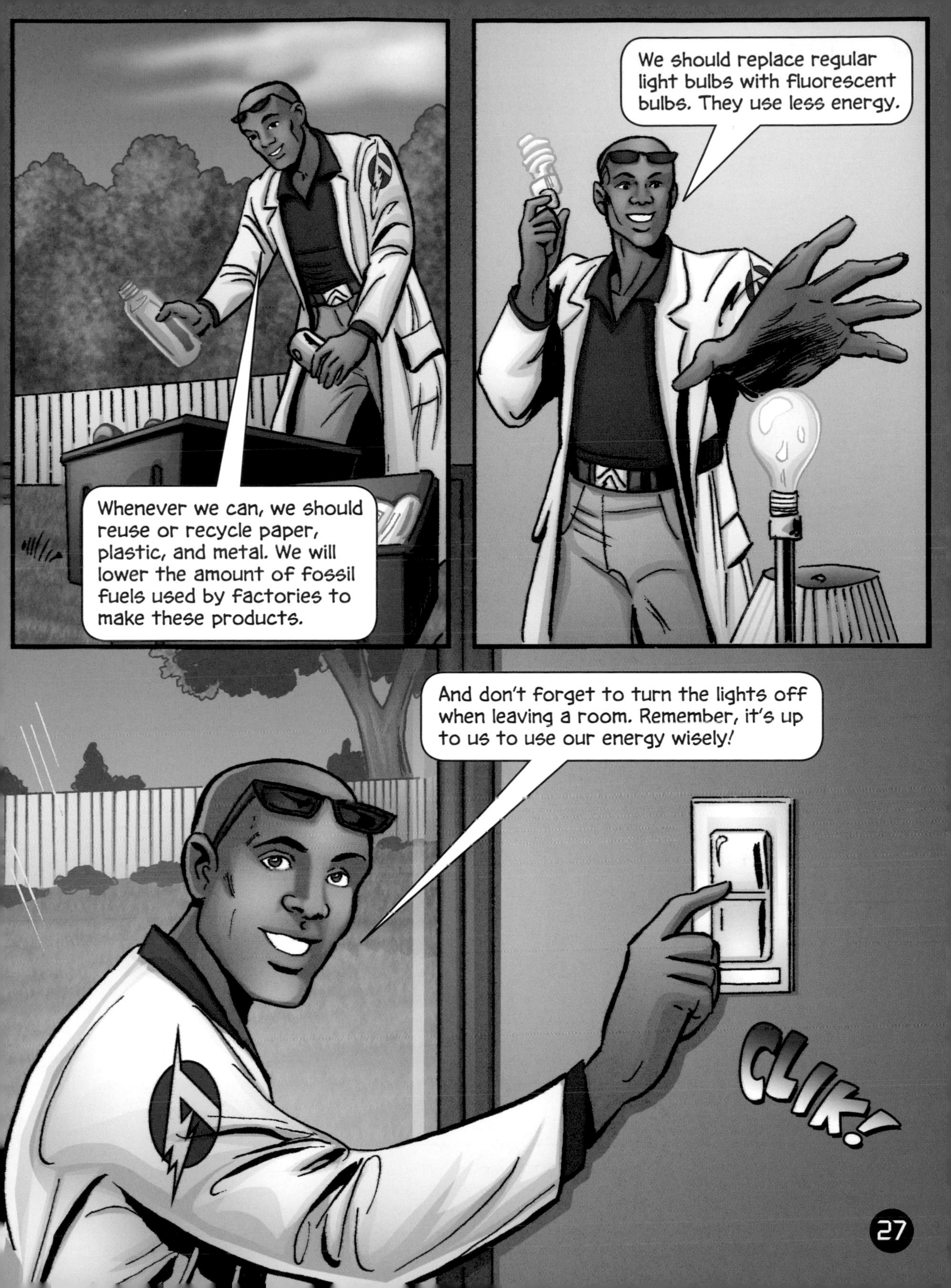
Whenever we can, we should reuse or recycle paper, plastic, and metal. We will lower the amount of fossil fuels used by factories to make these products.
We should replace regular light bulbs with fluorescent bulbs. They use less energy.
And don't forget to turn the lights off when leaving a room. Remember, it's up to us to use our energy wisely!
CLIK!

MORE ABOUT ENERGY

Fire was probably the first great energy invention. For thousands of years, people burned wood as their main source of fuel for heat, cooking, and other uses.

There is a whole family of energy called electromagnetic radiation. It includes gamma rays, X-rays, ultraviolet light, visible light, infrared light, microwaves, and radio waves. Visible light, however, is the only form we can see with our eyes. Some animals, like bees, can see ultraviolet light too.

The color of light we see gives us information about its energy level. A rainbow's colors are always in the same order: red, orange, yellow, green, blue, indigo, and violet. The colors are also arranged in order of increasing energy. Red light has lower energy than green light. And violet light has the highest energy of all visible light.

Even though we can't see X-rays, we can use them to take images of the insides of our bodies. X-rays allow us to see beneath the skin down to our bones.

Nothing in the universe can move faster than light. Light moves at a blistering 186,000 miles (300,000 kilometers) per second. A beam of light can travel around the world seven times in just one second.

Some scientists think the universe is filled with an invisible and mysterious force called dark energy. They believe dark energy is causing the universe to expand at an accelerating rate.

A huge amount of energy holds atoms together. In nuclear power plants, energy is released when atoms are split apart to create smaller atoms. This is called nuclear fission. In the sun, energy is produced when atoms are combined, or fused, together. This process is called nuclear fusion.

Almost half of the energy consumed by Americans in their homes is used for space heating. Another quarter is used for lighting and appliances. The rest is used for refrigeration, air conditioning, and heating water.

ENERGY COASTER

Experiment with potential and kinetic
energy with your very own roller coaster!

WHAT YOU NEED:

- scissors
- 3 feet (91 centimeters) of
  foam pipe insulation
- duct tape
- table
- books
- plastic cup
- marble

WHAT YOU DO:

1. Cut the full length of foam pipe insulation in half. When done, you will have
   two U-shaped pieces of foam.

2. Tape the U-shaped pieces of foam end to end to create one long track.

3. Tape one end of the track to the edge of a table. This will be the start of your
   roller coaster.

4. Angle the track down from the edge of the table. Then use books to create
   hills and curves along the length to make a roller coaster track.

5. Tape a plastic cup to the very end of the roller coaster track.

6. Release a marble at the start of the track. Watch as the marble's potential
   energy turns into kinetic energy when it rolls down the track.

7. Did the marble make it all the way down the track and into the cup? If not,
   experiment with the features of your roller coaster. Add more pipe insulation
   to make the track longer. Change the angle of the start or the size of the
   hills. Adjust the shape of the curves or even add a loop. Find the best way to
   harness the power of potential and kinetic energy on your roller coaster.

DISCUSSION QUESTIONS

1. What is the difference between potential energy and kinetic energy? Give an example of each to support your answer.

2. What is the law of the conservation of energy? Think of an example of how you see this law in action every day.

3. What are some common examples of fossil fuels? What are the advantages and disadvantages to using them as energy sources?

4. Why is it important for everyone to save energy? What are some simple ways in which we can do so?

WRITING PROMPTS

1. Make a list of the types of energy mentioned in this book. Then write a paragraph explaining which one you like the best and why.

2. Draw a diagram that shows how energy moves from the sun, through nature, and to you in an energy chain. Label where heat energy is lost between each link in the chain.

3. Much of our energy comes from burning fossil fuels. But what would happen if we ran out of coal, oil, and natural gas? Write a short story detailing how our world would change, for better or worse, if we ran out of fossil fuels.

4. Max highlights a number of renewable energy sources. Pick one and write a persuasive argument for why we should use that energy source more.

TAKE A QUIZ!

GLOSSARY

Calorie (KA-luh-ree)—a measurement of the amount of energy that food gives you

electromagnetic radiation (i-lek-troh-mag-NET-ik ray-dee-AY-shuhn)—electromagnetic waves of all different lengths; electromagnetic radiation ranges from short gamma rays to long radio waves

electron (i-LEK-tron)—a tiny particle in an atom that travels around the nucleus

generator (JEN-uh-ray-tur)—a machine that makes electricity by turning a magnet inside a coil of wire

gravity (GRAV-uh-tee)—a force that pulls objects with mass together; gravity pulls objects down toward the center of earth

insulation (in-suh-LAY-shuhn)—a material that stops heat, sound, or cold from entering or escaping

joule (JOOL)—a unit of work or energy

kinetic energy (ki-NET-ik EN-ur-jee)—the energy of a moving object

molecule (MOL-uh-kyool)—the atoms making up the smallest unit of a substance

potential energy (puh-TEN-shuhl EN-ur-jee)—the stored energy of an object that is raised, stretched, or squeezed

radiation (ray-dee-AY-shuhn)—a form of energy, such as heat, light, X-rays, microwaves, or radio waves; radiation also includes dangerous, high-energy nuclear radiation

resistance (ri-ZISS-tuhnss)—a force that opposes or slows the motion of an object; friction is a form of resistance

READ MORE

Batchelor, Jacob. *Energy.* A True Book. New York: Scholastic Inc., 2019.

Petersen, Kristen. *Understanding Kinetic Energy.* Mastering Physics. New York: Cavendish Square Publishing, 2015.

Peterson, Megan Cooley. *Scooby-Doo! A Science of Energy Mystery: The High-Voltage Ghost.* Scooby-Doo Solves It with S.T.E.M. North Mankato, Minn.: Capstone Press, 2016.

Spilsbury, Richard. *Investigating Forces and Motion.* Investigating Science Challenges. New York: Crabtree Publishing, 2018.

INTERNET SITES

Use Facthound to find Internet sites related to this book.

Visit *www.facthound.com*

Just type in 9781543558739 and go!

INDEX